WHAT

SHE

DOESN'T

KNOW

...will kill her

WHAT

SHE

DOESN'T

KNOW

IF ONLY SHE KNEW MYSTERY SERIES
BOOK 3

PAMELA CRANE

Tabella House
Raleigh, North Carolina

Thank you for supporting authors and literacy by purchasing this book. Want to add more gripping reads to your library? As the author of more than a dozen award-winning and bestselling books, you can find all of Pamela Crane's works on her website at www.pamelacrane.com.

This is for all women who have ever felt too old or too young; too outspoken or too quiet; too weird or too vanilla; unpretty or shallow; boring or a pipe dreamer; cast aside or controlled:

You are never too much of you. Like a raw gem, you may be rough around the edges, covered in dirt, but you are perfect in your imperfections and more valuable than musgravite (and if you don't know what that is, keep reading the book...).

Note to the Reader

If you're new to the IF ONLY SHE KNEW MYSTERY SERIES, welcome to the town of Bloodson Bay, where the people are strange but the rising body count is even stranger. I hope you'll stay awhile… but I'll warn you now: it's got a *Hotel California* vibe going on. Once you visit, you may never leave.

If you're a long-term resident of this villain-filled village with more ups and downs than a pregnant woman's mood swings, then I'm glad to see you've survived… so far! And boy do I have a treat for you for hanging in there.

But before we get our hands bloody—I mean *dirty*—I'd like to share a little background information about the characters that made this book so much fun to write.

Inspired by some extra-awesome real-life friends, Ginger Mallowan (named after Agatha Christie's married surname), Sloane Apara, and Tara *Christie* (take a wild guess who she's named after) are particularly unforgettable and special to me. You may have noticed the Agatha Christie-themed names, a tribute to my appreciation of the Queen of Crime, and if you didn't notice that, then I have a feeling you will probably not solve the mystery in the upcoming pages, since I did pretty much just spell it out for you.

About the cast: In this book our lead character is Ginger.

And she is, well, *Ginger*—a big-hearted Southerner who is always good for a laugh. She's loosely based a close friend of mine who is as spunky as she is whip-smart. As a mom during the 1980s, her quirky personality comes out in her vintage wardrobe and music tastes, which I happen to appreciate. Even though her vision is failing and her bones creak more than they used to, she's as vibrant and steadfast as a North Carolinian summer sun. And much like the sun, she always shows up.

Sloane, in particular, comes into her own in this book, as her Nigerian Deaf backstory was lovingly filled in by a friend of mine who shares many of Sloane's experiences as a Deaf Nigerian-American immigrant. Sloane's real-life alter-ego gave me the courage to write a character I was worried I'd misrepresent, but I'm glad I heeded her advice to include her. As my dear friend keeps reminding me, the more we try to understand the lives of others, the deeper we build our own humanity, empathy, and character.

Tara, last but not least and appointed "leader" of *Tara's Angels,* took a little back seat in this book in order to let her friends shine. Because Tara knows that being a good friend means supporting one another, even if it calls us to step out of the spotlight and put our friends' needs before our own once in a while.

What makes the town of Bloodson Bay so fun for me to live in—I mean *write about*, because certainly I know the difference between fiction and reality—is not just the quirky characters, but the decades I get to explore and bring to life in each book. If you've read the whole series so far, you probably noticed how I choose a different era for each story in the series:

The prequel *If Only She Knew* takes us all the way back to

the 1830s, to the origins of Bloodson Bay and how it got its infamous name.

The 1980s Reagan Era are explored in book 1, *Little Does She Know*, where I got to relive big hair and Madonna. (Did either ever really go out of style?)

Growing up in the 1990s, I couldn't resist bringing out the Gangsta Rap, backwards jeans, and Grunge Scene we all know and love, found in book 2, *She Knows Too Much*.

Where are we headed to this time in book 3? *What She Doesn't Know* (will kill her) transports you back to the Disco Era of the 1970s, so I hope you've got your groove ready to do a little dance, make a little love, and solve a lot of murder tonight!

WHAT SHE DOESN'T KNOW

BLOODSON BAY BULLETIN

December 3, 1979

WOMEN BOOKKEEPERS NEEDED!

Exciting new careers in bookkeeping are giving thousands of lonely women like you a new outlook on life. And you don't have to be smart to get started!

Everything is explained by experts in easy-to-understand language. We train you at home in <u>your</u> spare time, and your <u>husband</u> won't even miss dinner. You get an automatic electric adding machine and an instant-action pocket-size electronic calculator so you don't have to worry about being good at arithmetic.

<u>Was</u> your shot at a career ruined by your <u>kids</u>? Don't feel <u>ill</u> about <u>bad</u> luck! <u>You</u> <u>are</u> the perfect candidate. Take the <u>next</u> step to becoming a bookkeeper today!

I wasn't sure what offended me more—the implication that women were bored and lonely math-illiterate idiots, or that someone felt that *I* in particular needed to hear this. Not that it

5

mattered. This antiquated newspaper advertisement was not just some anti-woman propaganda from the seventies. It was an intentional, cryptic message for me… and it wasn't the first one I had gotten, either.

"What's it say, Ginger?"

I felt a chin rest on my shoulder and the scent of garlic invade my nose. Tara Christie—my best friend and daughter-in-law, go figure that they could be one and the same!—nudged aside my personal space as her breath warmed my ear.

I sniffed.

"Caesar salad for lunch, Tara?" I guessed, shrugging her heavy head off of my collarbone.

"How'd you know?" Tara cupped her hand over her mouth, exhaled, and smelled her breath.

"Darlin'. Your breath could peel the shell off a crawdad."

Despite the decades of age difference between me and Tara, we went together like a deep-fryer and pickles. Only a true Southerner would appreciate that combo, which I was, through and through.

As neighbors and close friends for over sixteen years, we had test drove the conventional rules of in-law formality when Tara tried calling me *Mom* a few times. But after all those years as friends, the word never quite felt right for either of us, so we ditched convention and used our plain old names—Ginger and Tara. Unless Tara was taking too long to get ready for an outing, in which case I called her Little Miss Priss.

She didn't like that nickname much.

"It's another cryptic message," I said, searching for the telltale underlined letters and words from the yellowed newspaper ad that I knew would drop a clue regarding my husband's disappearance.

It wasn't his first vanishing act either, I might add. Let me explain:

It had all started back in April, a little more than five months ago, when my estranged husband, Rick, showed up on my front porch. I hadn't seen him since he walked out on me and our three boys thirty-seven years ago. So you could imagine how shocked I was to open the door and lay eyes on him after so long.

One would think he'd have brought flowers and chocolates (or maybe some banana puddin') for this long overdue reunion to win a girl's heart back, right? No, not my long-lost spouse. Instead, Rick brought a bloody, gushing abdominal wound that I had to hand stitch closed with a needle and "thread." I used biodegradable floss, the mint-flavored kind—it's extra painful when woven through skin. A little thank-you from me to him for all the pain he'd put me through… and forgetting to bring flowers and chocolates.

The whole flesh-sewing thing felt very Buffalo Bill from *Silence of the Lambs* as I threaded the wound. Rick had been tightlipped about what had happened to him, but I was certain he'd gotten stabbed by one of his many criminal associates. He swore up and down he had finally broken free from that life of crime.

Promises, promises.

Lies, lies.

To make a long story short, I agreed to give Rick another chance at a *real* marriage together. The kind of relationship where a couple can rely on each other, love each other, even fight with each other… as long as we were together. I knew it was a stupid decision on my part, I might add. But he was the kryptonite to my Superman. You wouldn't understand unless you knew him like I did.

Anyway, Rick and I had spent nearly every day together since April talking and canoodling, if you know what I mean, until he just up and disappeared again three days ago. When he never showed up for our anniversary date at Luna's Steak and Seafood Restaurant to celebrate exactly fifty years to the day since we'd first fallen in love, I had a feeling Rick returned to the place he always went—in the wind.

If these puzzling 1970's newspaper messages I had been getting were any indication of what happened to him, Rick hadn't left on his own terms. Everything pointed to foul play.

"What's the message say?" Tara probed.

She didn't sound the least bit worried. Never one to hide how she felt, Tara hated Rick's guts like a cat hates water, or like I hated tourists crowding our town's beaches. But still… Tara could at least pretend to be upset, for my sake.

"Hold your horses," I replied. "I'm still working on it."

Like the previous newspaper clippings I had received, I pieced the mysterious message together that I suspected delivered more bad news that meant my estranged husband's life was in dire straits… or worse.

By worse I meant *dead*.

The letters bounced and bobbed as I trembled. Holding the page out far enough to clear up the blurred words that the pair of cheaters in my purse could fix, I was too anxious—and prideful—to root around for them. Eventually the words came together:

your husband was k ill d you are next

"*Your husband was ill. You are next,*" I whispered, repeating the marked words verbatim. "Lord have mercy, Rick's sick! And it's contagious! Do you think whatever he has is deadly?"

"Huh?" Tara pulled the clipping from my fingers and read it. "Oh, honey, that can't be what that says."

Tara wrapped her arm around me as the shudders worked their way up my hands to my entire body. I didn't know where the heebie-jeebies stopped and the age-onset tremors began.

"I told you to get your eyes checked. Why won't you get some eyeglasses?"

"I don't need them. I can spot a tick on a coon hound from a country mile."

I had always prided myself on my 20/20 eagle-eye vision, the better to keep a lookout on our neighborhood. Only recently had I noticed my neighborhood *watch* was turning into a neighborhood *squint*. I hadn't told Tara about my drugstore cheaters, lest she demand I give up my position as Head Watcher. And in case you're wondering, yes, I made up the term and it suits me just fine, no matter how weird it sounds *watching heads*.

"Well, then you'd clearly see that it says…" Tara paused, silently reading the message. "Oh. I'm so sorry, Ging."

"Why? What's the bad news?"

Tara refused to meet my gaze as she mumbled, "Your husband was *killed*."

"What the—? No, that can't be."

The shock of reality—that Rick was dead, gone, for good this time—grazed me but didn't fully hit me yet. I had been so used to imagining him as a stiff countless times in the past, especially when he would empty our bank account at the bar or forget to pick our son Benson up from school while I was working... but *imagining* and *knowing* were two very different things.

"Do you think this is talking about Rick..." Tara hesitated as she caught herself speaking the unspeakable, "or do you think this is referring to Chris?" A panicked pitch lifted her voice at the thought of her husband being the intended target.

Normally my mind wouldn't have even considered that possibility. But today wasn't normal. In fact, quite the opposite when Chris, her husband and my son, hadn't come home on the flight scheduled to arrive earlier this afternoon. A bomb threat, Tara found out, but the airline wouldn't give her any other information, as it was still under investigation. And the news hadn't reported on it yet, which meant anything could have happened.

Tara had tried calling Chris countless times, all of which went straight to voicemail. Unlike his negligent bio-dad Rick, Chris always showed up for his family. Always. No bomb threat could keep him away. At least I hoped not.

Could Chris have been killed? No, I couldn't imagine my straight-laced, innocent son being punished for his father's shady business dealings. It couldn't be Chris. It had to be Rick. It just *had* to be.

"No, honey, don't think like that," I tried to sooth Tara. And myself. "There's no way this is talking about Chris. I'm sure he's fine. Probably throwing back rum and cokes at the airport bar."

Which Chris never would do because he had the alcohol tolerance of a four-year-old. And I only knew about childhood alcohol tolerance because Rick had once left an open bottle of vodka out and our four-year-old Bennie had mistaken it for water. One gulp was all he needed to realize the water had gone "bad" and he never liked drinking water much since.

Tara stumbled back, tears filling her eyes. "But that's what criminals do! They target the loved ones. They could have gotten to Chris in order to make Rick do something for them!"

To make Rick do what? There was no ransom demand, no orders, nothing. Just threats. Maybe even empty ones.

"Whoever it is, it's probably just an intimidation tactic. I mean, these are criminals we're dealing with. They're professional liars. I'm sure Chris is fine. And Rick too."

But I didn't believe a darn in the yarn I was spinning. Because if Rick had been abducted by who I suspected was behind this, he didn't think twice about pulling the trigger.

WHAT SHE DOESN'T KNOW

Part 1
Ginger Mallowan

WHAT SHE DOESN'T KNOW

Chapter 1

Three Days Earlier…

It would have been the perfect day, if not for how it ended. Like a scenic drive through the autumn-colored mountains, only to take one wrong turn that sent you over a cliff Thelma and Louise style. Or cozied up by a fire with a hot cup of coffee on a cold night, only to spill it on your lap and get second-degree burns. The day started with my world so perfectly whole… if only I would have sensed the earthquake rumbling before it split it in half.

My toes tingled from the cool sand as the September sun settled into the horizon behind us. Dancing to the sound of pelicans prattling, my husband held me against him as the ocean patted the beach with loving touches. For the first time in years I felt young again. Vibrant.

And exposed, as a breeze lifted the hem of my dress, sending a prickle of chills up my legs.

"It's windier than a sack full of farts," I commented, holding the skirt down.

"Don't hide those legs." Rick pinched my rear, making me giggle like a schoolgirl with a secret. "Those are my favorite things about you."

"My legs—really?" I scoffed. "And what if I lost my legs,

would you still want to be with me?"

He chuckled, clearly enjoying this game of *What If.*

"As long as you never lose this butt…" He gave my rear a playful squeeze, then pressed his lips to my ear while we swayed in lazy circles, his stubble scratching my cheek.

"You need to shave," I commented, playing aloof.

That only made Rick rub his scruffy chin all over my face and neck. His mouth lingered near my collarbone. I instantly went weak.

"And you need to shut that pretty mouth up and let me kiss you," he murmured against the wrinkles of my skin that had thinned to tissue paper over the years. I loved how Rick didn't seem to notice. "Did I tell you how beautiful you look tonight?"

"A couple times," I confirmed.

For the first time in years, I *did* feel beautiful, which was a hard feat after I hit sixty-five. It'd be a good thing for Rick to remember that, too, if he had any chance of coming home with me tonight. Even though he was technically my husband, as far as I was concerned Rick was still on a trial basis earning his place in my bed. I'd warned him: one slip-up and I'd send him packing. For good reason.

As much as I tried, I could never fully get over what Rick Mallowan did to me thirty-seven years ago. After he had abandoned me and our two kids, with a third on the way, I'd be lying if I said single motherhood of rambunctious boys and a dead-end job didn't leave me feeling empty most days. Depressed. And prematurely gray.

What woman doesn't want someone to support her and make her feel wanted? So like any hot-blooded woman in the Excess Eighties, I filled in the empty spaces with whatever I could for as long as I could.

My thirties were brimming with attention from Tan-tastic 'Roid Ragers who wore too-tight cropped white t-shirts that made their fake tans look orange. While the *Dynasty*-era George Hamilton look might appear okay from afar, don't dare let him sweat on you at the nightclub, unless you plan to soak your clothes in stain remover to get out those faux tan lines.

After hitting forty, I exchanged my spandex for Guess jeans, drawing the attention of Mr. Flash with the Cash, the typical narcissist who invested more in building his Wall Street portfolio than his character. I learned quickly that no number of free drinks on his Amex was worth a night of egocentric conversation about his penthouse… and yacht… and beachfront property… and I never made it past that before excusing myself to the bathroom, where I'd slip out the window and never look back.

By the time I turned fifty and Y2K had come and gone, the male gaze dwindled down to the uncomfortable stares from the Local Drunk. He was always outgoing enough to introduce himself through a slur of cliché compliments, but too plastered to get my name right.

Finally when sixty arrived, I happily bid farewell to that long-dormant lust for male companionship. I settled into an unfamiliar but welcome norm of ho's over bro's, shaking my head at the naïve up-and-coming youth who would one day make the same woeful trek through the male species as I had.

I didn't envy youth or long for its return. I liked who I was— they didn't call them *fine* lines for nothing!—and I appreciated the wisdom that only comes with age. If only I could have warned myself back then.

But a shadow of that yearning for male affirmation—Rick's affirmation, specifically—resurfaced tonight. Tonight marked the fifty-year anniversary of when we had both said those three magic words to each other: *"I love you,"* from my lips, followed by *"You foxy mama,"* from Rick's lips (to which he ended with an obligatory *"I love you too"*).

Tonight he delivered all that affection and more on a silver platter full of compliments and handsy touches.

"I can hardly keep my paws off you, you look so good." His bold fingers roamed my body, and I didn't stop him. Yet.

I *did* look darn good. I had left nothing on the table before walking out the front door to meet Rick this afternoon, as I swiped my mouth with a Madonna-circa-1985 cherry red lipstick—my signature lip color.

After spending almost an hour trying on different outfits, I finally settled on a lip-matching red dress that skimmed my knees. Men loved a woman in red—heck, a love song and movie were based on it, so it had to be true. While I knew the rule of thumb warning against redheads wearing red, Rick seemed to approve the look as his palm rested on the small of my back.

"You're lucky you don't have to keep those hands to yourself," I said with a wink, grabbing his wrist and shifting it down to my rear. "You don't look too shabby yourself."

The decades that we had been apart were apparent in the way his skin sagged, but looking at him now, seeing the glow of his face and sparkle in his brown eyes, I would never have guessed he had been worn down by the stress of God-knows-what-crime all those years.

Except I knew of his crimes.

And it weighed on me.

I was married to a criminal. Even worse, one who had gotten away with it. Sometimes I didn't know how he slept at night… at least not without his orange bottle of sleeping pills.

Only God knew the lives Rick had destroyed along the way—mine and our three boys, for starters—and yet he got off scot-free. It didn't sit right with me that he had never turned himself in, but I didn't like the idea of the man I loved getting locked behind bars either, where he would most certainly rot until his dying breath if the cops ever found out just how deep in it he had been.

Had been. Or maybe *still was.* I had never really gotten an honest-to-God answer if Rick had left his life of crime behind him or not.

Suddenly I felt queasy. Nervous. Antsy to get away from him.

So much for our happy reunion.

Rick must have noticed me stiffen, because he earnestly met my eyes.

"You okay?" he asked.

"I'm just anxious, is all. I have a lot on my mind."

"I've got a pill for that," he joked.

"No thanks. I'm sure you need every last one of your Xanax." I didn't want the same pills that helped him forget what he had done.

"I know I've said it before, Gingersnap, but I'm sorry." He squeezed me gently, and I nearly liquefied in his arms. He had that power over me, to draw a forgiveness that I didn't want to give. "I'll forever be sorry for what I put you and the boys through. But I'm gonna make it right. I swear. For as long as I live, I'll prove I was worth waiting for."

I stopped swaying in step with him and pulled away. "You think I was *waiting* for you all these years?"

The gall of him to assume I put my life on hold for him! Even if I kind of did, he should have never suspected it! As if I couldn't have moved on if I wanted to.

"Well… you're still single," he said. "Legally married… to me. Doesn't that mean you were waiting for me?"

Now I was pissed that he dared think my pathetic, lonely life revolved around him while he was off galivanting and living it up.

"No, my marital status had nothing to do with waiting for you." I angrily crossed my arms. "I couldn't divorce a man who wasn't around to sign the papers."

"I'm sure you could have, Ginger. But you didn't."

True, he got me there. I had never made the effort to start the paperwork, and over the years I never asked myself why. Maybe it was out of pure laziness, or maybe I held on to that flicker of a flame that refused to extinguish. But I would never let Rick know that.

"I didn't file for divorce because I had no desire to marry again. And yes, in case you're wondering, I *did* date. Lots of men. Countless men!"

I wasn't sure why I was making myself out to be the Hoochie Mama Tramp of Bloodson Bay. Quite the opposite, in fact. But I felt like I had to prove myself to Rick, that I could have gotten—and did get—any man I wanted.

His jaw twitched, then tightened. Ah, there was the jealousy I was hoping for!

"Why didn't you want to remarry if you had all these men ogling you?"

I shrugged. "I was done having kids, so what was the point in tying myself to another guy who'd let me down? And let the boys down?"

He winced. I was glad it hurt.

"I deserve that," he finally said. "I know I can't make up for missing out on Benson, Cole, and Chris's lives."

And Bennie's death, I wanted to correct him.

Rick's absenteeism as a parent was evident in the way he still couldn't remember that Cole now went by the name Jonah. Or the fact that Chris was married to my best friend Tara. Sometimes I felt like Rick made the minimum effort possible to invest in our lives over the past six months.

"It wasn't like I wanted to stay away from you, Gingersnap. I couldn't be with you because…" Silence hung between us for far too long.

"Why? It sure felt like you were hiding from me."

"That wasn't my intention. I've always been *around*—"

"Yeah, yeah. As you say, the best place to hide is in plain sight. Maybe if you stick around this time you can at least try to get to know your sons."

Though I doubted it. Even I hadn't restored my relationship with Chris due to giving him up for adoption days after his birth. We had Rick to thank for that too, after I realized I couldn't raise a third baby on my own.

"That's my plan, Gingersnap, and my promise. To win you all back."

Part of me wanted to laugh at his weak *promise*. He'd left us for so long, and I still hadn't gotten the full story of what he'd spent the past forty years doing exactly. Not that I wanted details. It was something criminal, and that's all I needed to know.

The sky was growing dark, along with my mood.

"I think it's time I head home. I don't want to spoil our time with talk about the past." I picked up the blanket we had picnicked on and shoved it into my beach bag. Grabbing my jelly sandals, I slipped into them and began heading to my car.

"I'm guessing I lost my shot at spending the night with you?" Rick asked, grabbing his own shoes and following me in a hurry.

Rick had spent more nights in my bed than not since his return. But tonight I needed space.

"Not tonight."

"Are we still on for dinner later?" he asked as I kept walking. "It's a special night."

All week I had been looking forward to celebrating the fifty-year anniversary of when we'd first fallen in love as newly-minted adults, sitting across from each other at Luna's Steak and Seafood Restaurant, the oldest and fanciest place one could get surf 'n' turf in Bloodson Bay. Back in 1973 we had been young and broke, but he had spoiled me with his entire meager savings of $32 that night, and I decided then and there I was going to tame the bad boy with the tattoos and leather jacket and motorcycle that my parents had forbidden me from seeing.

"Yes, we're still on for supper. I just need to run home and freshen up, then I'll meet you there," I said, slightly out of breath.

Rick caught up to me as I reached my car parked past the dunes in a crumbling parking lot with weeds poking up through the broken cement.

"You sure you don't want me to pick you up? Give you a

ride on *Large Marge* for old times' sake?"

Large Marge was the name he'd given his motorcycle, which had been chosen by four-year-old Bennie after Rick had taken him to see *Pee-wee's Big Adventure* at the movie theater. While the motorcycles had come and gone over the years, the nickname stuck with each bike, and it stuck on Bennie too after Rick started calling him his little Pee-wee any time they'd go for a motorcycle ride.

"When pigs fly! I'll make a deal with you. I'll get on a motorcycle with you when you come to church with me."

I smirked, already knowing his answer. Rick had insisted more than once that he'd burst into flames if he ever set foot in a holy place. I didn't doubt it.

"I guess I'll meet you at Luna's then," he acquiesced.

I popped open the trunk and tossed my beach bag in beside a cardboard box I had never had the emotional strength to deal with. *Benson Mallowan Donation for Loving Arms Children's Home* was written across the side in black marker, in a handwriting that I missed terribly.

"You've had that in there forever," Rick commented. "Want me to drop it off at the donation center for you?"

He was trying to make amends, and it thawed me just a little.

"No, that's okay… I still need to go through it all."

"I already did," Rick said, reaching for the box. "It's nothing but junk."

"I said no!" I yelled, the words flying out like darts.

"Geez, sorry. I was just trying to be helpful."

I didn't know how to explain why that box still sat in my trunk. Or why I couldn't make myself drop it off. But the look of despair on Rick's face made me want to at least try.

"I didn't mean to yell. The box… Bennie put it in here right before he died. I never had the courage to get rid of it. It reminds me of him. A lot of his old clothes and random stuff are in there."

"Oh, Gingersnap, I didn't know."

"How could you? It was over a year and a half ago. I don't know why I haven't gotten rid of it yet. It's pathetic, isn't it?"

"Not at all. He's your son. There's no statute of limitations on how long you're allowed to grieve."

My grief had been a mixed bag. Bennie could be a real selfish piece of work, plotting to toss me in a *retirement home*, he called it, so that he could get his grubby hands on my house. He unexpectedly died before he could carry it out. But I still loved him and missed him fiercely. That was what motherhood was all about—our kids testing the depths of our love and always passing, no matter how deep or dark it got.

The beginnings of healing eventually came when Sloane Apara, Bennie's ex-wife who I only finally grew close with after his death, offered to start a memorial fund in his honor. The goal was to support more Deaf services in Bloodson Bay, with hopes of attracting Deaf residents into our Deaf-friendly community. Sloane, who had lost her hearing as a child after a life-threatening bout of meningitis, funded the memorial and had already gotten in contact with a few families looking to relocate here. My son had done a lot of bad things, but together Sloane and I hoped to rectify those wrongs in our own unique way.

"I know I need to move on. Starting with this box." I would give myself just one more feel of Bennie's clothes, one more smell of his shirts, and then I would let it go.

Rick wrapped an arm around me, hugging me before

heading to his motorcycle parked beside me, where a puddle of oil collected from the faulty oil pan gasket he had yet to fix.

"Healing from a loss like that takes one day at a time, right?"

I smiled and nodded as Rick revved his bike and drove away. Just like healing from your estranged husband's dark past took one day at a time… if healing was even possible when the past couldn't stay buried.

Chapter 2

Tables for two, aglow with flickering candles and decorated with tiny vases of flowers, dotted the dining room on the other side of the tinted window of Luna's Steak and Seafood Restaurant. A distant memory pulled me in as I caught my reflection against the brown glass. At this very restaurant, exactly fifty years ago to the day, I fell in love for the first—and only—time.

I had been young and passionate and maybe even a little— or a lot, if I'm being honest—boy crazy when I agreed to let bad-boy Rick Mallowan take me out on a date. But passion and craziness were a birthright of the young, weren't they?

Rick was the kid who never graduated high school, and he instantly met my parents' disapproval from the moment they saw his Bee Gees-inspired red leather jacket—which was probably stolen, my dad insisted—and his tacky gold medallion necklace—which was too flashy for a boy his age, my mom grumbled. Despite the parental warnings, the love felt was as real as a blade to the heart—and that's exactly what Rick ended up doing to me. Gutting me.

But I was a believer in second chances, and this evening was a night of do-overs.

Dressed to the nines, Rick had left me at the beach parking

lot, reminding me to meet him at seven o'clock sharp while he ran some errands beforehand.

"You remember where we had our first date, right?" he had teased as he revved his motorcycle.

"You know I do. My memory isn't *that* bad," I had replied.

How could I ever forget? All these years later, a fluster still warmed my cheeks as I recalled the way he had looked at me from across the table, and the way my blood pulsed only for him.

Tonight was an elaborate—and oh-so-romantic—scheme to rekindle the flame we had sparked so long ago. Rick thoughtfully booked the same table for two at Luna's, where as youngin's we had sat gazing at each other and slipping into hours-long conversation on a date that lasted through morning as we ended it with all-you-can-eat waffles at Debbie's Diner along with the sunrise.

Tucked under my arm was a scrapbook collection of golden memories, only good ones, as a peace offering.

On the inside of the cover I had glued a photocopy of our marriage certificate:

This certifies that Ginger Boyle and Rick Mallowan were united in marriage on the 30th day of April in the year of our Lord 1974.

Filling the interior pages were faded love notes we had left each other over the years, taped on the bathroom mirror, fridge, and even inside the oven when Rick would surprise me with takeout for supper. After the invention of Post-It notes in 1977, our messages grew more colorful, frequent, and hidden in the craziest of places, like the time I almost drank one that had been stuck inside my coffee cup. Almost every square inch of our home had been marked by our passionate prose.

Alternating with the notes, photographed images captured sepia nights where we had danced barefoot in the kitchen, another caught a black-and-white blurry shot during an impromptu road trip to catch the Who live in concert. I even managed to find an elusive picture of the time we snuck into Studio 54, where I brushed elbows with *the* Diana Ross!

Those were the pre-kid days of the 1970s when Rick and I were wild and carefree. All I wanted was to return to that place, and we were so close to getting there. Tonight would seal it for sure, I thought.

A heady rush of adrenalin quickened my heart as I cast one last approving look at myself in the glass and opened the door. It swooshed shut behind me as I approached the hostess podium.

I had spent an hour touching up my gray roots and staining the bathroom tub red. Another perfecting my makeup, lining my lips in my signature cherry lipstick and my green eyes in pale blue eyeshadow. I felt as fantabulous as I did nervous.

"Do you have a reservation?" the hostess asked as I approached, tossing her blond hair over her shoulder with a flair.

"It's under the name Rick Mallowan," I answered.

"Yes, ma'am. Follow me, please."

I hummed along to the soft sound of "Escape" by Rupert Holmes—I knew it as "The Pina Colada Song"—that filled the restaurant as she led me to a table with a bouquet of pink carnations in the center. They looked just like the gas station flowers Rick had brought on our first date in 1973, an extravagance that had impressed me back then as a small-town girl who had never gotten flowers from a boy before.

A wrapped gift box sat at the place setting opposite me. I sat and examined the box, imagining what could be inside. It was a little large for an engagement ring, but around the right size and shape for a necklace. Well butter my butt and call me a biscuit, I was getting jewelry!

Seven o'clock came and went, and I loved my husband.

By a quarter after seven the waitress brought me warm biscuits and cinnamon butter, along with a glass of their house wine while I worried over Rick's delay.

By seven forty-five I was annoyed with Rick and embarrassed as I downed three more glasses and had eaten all but two of the biscuits, which I wrapped in a napkin and tucked into my purse, regretting that I couldn't take the cinnamon butter too.

By eight o'clock, after six unanswered texts to Rick and several pitying looks from the waitstaff, I hated his guts.

Under normal circumstances I would have chalked up the tardiness to Rick being the disappearing act that he naturally was. But the box… he had planted it, along with the symbolic pink carnations, where his plate of surf 'n' turf should have been.

It begged me to open it. I considered waiting a little longer, then wondered if whatever was inside had something to do with his no-show. Was this an elaborate romantic scavenger hunt that I had already bungled by not opening it right away?

I eagerly pulled the ribbon, loosening the bow. The silk dropped to the table as I lifted the lid. But no fancy necklace was inside. No cutesy scavenger hunt. In fact, I had no idea what I was looking at as I lifted it up, examining it. But something told me life and death depended on me figuring it out.

Chapter 3

BLOODSON BAY BULLETIN
February 15, 1978

AVON REPRESENTATIVE WANTED

*Looking for classy, self-motivated, well-kept women
to handle increasing supply and demand. Must be willing
to learn and have available schedule. Sales skills needed.
Contact Mick for general details.*

Inside the box I found the darndest thing: an old newspaper
article. The clipping appeared to be an ad from the 1978
classifieds. I briefly recalled Rick and I sitting at our breakfast
nook, each of us searching through the *Bloodson Bay Bulletin*
wanted ads, a twenty-something broke couple looking for odd
jobs, circling the ones we liked.

Avon representative had not been one of my choices. I had
the sales tact of a toboggan store opening up in Florida, so I
mostly stuck to waitressing and cashier jobs, while Rick
eventually settled for an auto mechanic position that he hated.

I still didn't get the relevance of my… gift, if I could call it that. Had Don Draper written this sexist garbage? After reading it a second time, I noticed randomly underlined letters that seemed to spell out a message.

I glanced at the date at the top: February 15, 1978.

It was a familiar date, significant even, but I couldn't pin down exactly why. While Rick's idea of romance was motorcycle rides on long stretches of highway, or a Cheese Whiz and crackers picnic, I had never seen this side of him, sending me cryptic messages. Rick always cut to the chase, and his notes rarely strayed from being related to sex or supper, such as:

To my dy-no-mite doll, get your groove ready for tonight!

Or:

Dessert is on me, foxy lady.

(And by *dessert*, he meant whipped cream—literally on him.)

What kind of nonsensical love note was this? Unless it wasn't a love note after all.

I turned over the ad and saw a name I instantly recognized:

ESCAPED MASS MURDERER TED BUNDY RECAPTURED

February 15th had been the date the infamous serial killer Ted Bundy was recaptured. But that wasn't the only reason it sounded so familiar. There was something more. Was it another anniversary of some kind? I pulled up distant memories of the seventies, full of pre-child-rearing reckless fun. Adventure. And a little danger, too.

Then it hit me. A tiny piece of an incident that had been a rude awakening to me back then. I hadn't realized just how momentous it was until now.

This wasn't a grand gesture at all. This was something much darker. I flipped open the scrapbook I had brought as a gift for Rick, pulling out the photo of our Studio 54 escapade where Diana Ross was unknowingly felt up by yours truly. Across the back of the photo I had written the date: February 15, 1978.

Studio 54 had been a crazy night of ups and downs. The ups clearly being bumping elbows with the Motown Maven. The downs, on the other hand, had hit a new low with Rick. We had returned to our cheap New York motel after grooving the night away, and while I disrobed my husband, a baggie of white powder fell out of his jacket pocket. Along with a stainless steel screen that I had no clue what it was for. It had taken more than a minute for everything to click, until I realized it was cocaine and a Screenz coke screen—and to this day I still never tried the drug or understood the screen's purpose.

Needless to say, that day I saw a side of Rick that scared me. Possessive of the drugs when I asked him to flush them down the toilet. Shrugging them off as no big deal. Refusing to tell me his supplier. It was all cloak-and-dagger as Rick stormed off into the Manhattan streets that night after our huge fight, and it was the day the secrets started building. They would continue to build into a wall that eventually separated us.

The sender knew, and the ad clearly had something to do with that night:

The memorable date.

This specific Avon advertisement.

Rummaging through my purse, I found a pen. Then I started to piece the underlined letters together, writing each one on a paper napkin:

r i c k i s m i s s i n g

"Rickismissing?" I muttered in a single breath. The message slowly congealed together. The gaps broke up the words: "Rick is missing!"

It created a dire message revealing that Rick was in trouble, but I instinctively knew that involving the cops would mean certain death. For him, for me, who knows? You can't predict what a crime boss would do to a rat these days. Not that I could have involved the police anyway, since I knew Rick was knee-deep into drug running for the past forty years and I had no desire to get on his boss's bad side.

What was a good girl in love with a bad boy to do? I was still in the process of figuring that out.

Then there was something else that caught my attention. The contact name associated with the ad—*Contact Mick*—couldn't be a coincidence when you figured in Rick's infatuation with Mick Jagger. Had Rick been scouring the ads for drug messages back then? Before the age of the dark web and burner phones, were criminals communicating via the classifieds?

I scanned the room, looking for anything suspicious in case the message delivery guy—or girl; I was all for gender equality in every job, even crime—was watching. The restaurant was packed with patrons, but none of them seemed to notice me, albeit the occasional sympathetic glance as I sat alone at a table for two.

Getting up and taking my scrapbook and the box with me, I headed to the hostess stand where the girl greeted me with a chipper smile. I held out the gift box.

"Did you see who left this at my table?"

She shook her head. "No, ma'am, sorry. It's been a busy night."

Of course it wouldn't be that easy. I walked back to my table, wondering what I was supposed to do next, who had left it, and why. When I flipped over the box, taped to the bottom was a tiny sliver of paper with a typed note:

> If you want a future with Rick, you will have to search through the past.

The air seeped out of my lungs, but I couldn't draw more in. I felt dizzy with a lack of oxygen along with a lack of answers.

What now? Certainly *someone* should have seen *something*. My gaze settled on the bartenders, both dressed in black and busily tending to customers. I hoped at least one of them might have noticed something. From my experience, bartenders tended to be observant, always knowing when you were one gulp away from needing another drink. And they usually knew all the gossip, as drunk patrons with loose lips poured out their secrets while the barkeep poured more alcohol.

I was on the verge of tears as I approached the bar.

"Can I get you a drink, ma'am?" the barkeep closest to me offered, looking sophisticated in all black from his collared shirt to his cowboy boots. His warm smile was slightly crooked due to a facial scar that made him interesting to me.

"Um, no thanks. I'm looking for someone. Did you happen to see who left this at my table?" I asked, barely getting the question out.

I pointed to where I had been sitting.

"Sorry, ma'am, I didn't. It's been a busy night."

"So I keep hearing." I sighed any remaining hope I had held in that this whole thing was just a tasteless joke.

I didn't want to wonder where Rick was anymore. I thought I had finally been done with all the questions, all the wondering, all the stress and worry about what my husband was doing after-hours, or if it would catch up to me and the boys. I was back in the ring, fighting the same demons I thought I had finally defeated. I didn't want a future with a man who would make me relive our painful past again and again. Let his crimes catch up to him, for all I care! Just leave me out of it!

The bartender lingered, as if waiting for me to spill my guts. His silver nametag sparkled against the low lighting.

"Gunther," I read aloud. "Is that your real name?"

He chuckled. "Yep, I'm afraid so. Gunther Jones. I think my parents had big plans for me to be a security guard or bouncer

36

when I grew up."

"Bartender is the next logical tough-guy step, isn't it?" I tried on a grin. It felt fake. "If it's any consolation, you don't look like a Gunther."

Unless a Gunther was rail thin with curly gray hair tied back in a ponytail. Cute, too, if you liked the clean-shaven type, which right now I did. The pale seam of healed skin that ran from his lip to his chin gave him a Gunthery mysterious edge, like he'd been in a lot of fights in his heyday.

"Now that you know my name, don't you think it'd be fair if I knew yours?" And apparently he had a smile that would melt butter.

"It's Ginger."

"A little on the nose, huh?" With a gentle caress he touched the split ends of my freshly-dyed red hair that were way overdue for a trim. His knuckles brushed my collarbone, sending a tiny zap of electricity through my body.

"My parents weren't very creative." I tapped my face where Gunther's scar would be. "Is there a story behind that?"

Luckily he didn't seem offended. "It's a long one. I'll tell you if you stay awhile."

The glistening rows of half-empty liquor bottles behind him suddenly felt awfully tempting. It would be nice to blot out this awful night... even if only for a few hours.

"You know what? Maybe I'll have that drink after all."

Without a word, Gunther began pouring various bottles into a glass, then handed me a minty green beverage.

"A grasshopper on the house. And by the way, he's an idiot for standing you up."

I cocked an eyebrow. "You're assuming I got stood up."

37

"Why else would a beautiful lady like you be at a bar alone?"

Beautiful lady? "Laying it on thick, aren't you? Maybe I like drinking alone."

"Well, I hate to break it to you, but I'll be thwarting your plans tonight because I'm not going anywhere."

I glanced at the crowded bar where the other barkeep, a woman in matching black, her flaxen hair pulled up in a tight bun, hastily poured drinks and handed them out. From my profile angle, I thought I recognized one of her customers.

"Shouldn't you be helping your co-worker serve drinks?" I asked.

"Nah, she won't mind." Gunther must have noticed my skepticism. "Watch." Gunther called to her, "Hey, Kat! Care if I take a quick break?"

A line of heads turned our way.

Ah, yes, there sat Leonard Valance, Tara's archenemy and her sister-in-law Peace's boyfriend. I would have felt bad for the guy, being born into the evil Valance family against his will, but I knew what kind of man he was. The kind who kept secrets from his own girlfriend—secrets that he should go to jail for.

The lady bartender barely glanced up from pouring Leonard another drink to shake her head at Gunther. "Really, G? Flirting on the job?"

Her accent was thick, but the bar was too noisy for me to place where she was from. Definitely not a Southerner.

"I think I'm needed here more," Gunther insisted, patting the glossy counter.

She laughed good-naturedly. "You owe me, G."

"Just add it to my tab," Gunther replied, then turned back to me. "As you were saying…"

"You'll probably get fired for this."

He shrugged. "Something tells me you're worth it."

"You got a cell phone number?" I ventured.

"Nope. No cell phone. I don't believe in modern technology."

"Oh, you're one of *those*."

"If you mean one of those smart, intelligent men who would love to talk to you the old-fashioned way via conversation over dinner and drinks, then yes, I'm one of *those*."

Gunther, clearly good at his job, would certainly be getting a nice tip tonight.

"Now about that scar story…" I prompted.

While I sipped the minty, creamy concoction, all thoughts of Rick and whatever mess he had gotten himself into disappeared down with the drink.

Chapter 4

The sun blinded me. My head throbbed. But the hangover was totally worth it.

Last night my new friend Gunther and I had closed down the bar together, talking the hours away about everything from our good ol' days to our bad life choices.

He listened as I admitted to my terrible judge of character when it came to men, and I laughed as he regaled me with his crazy stories when it came to women. Anyone who would attempt to rescue his ex-girlfriend's missing pet—mistaking a baby bobcat for her escaped housecat, only to come face-to-face with the mama bobcat and survive... and a facial scar to prove it—was worth hanging out with for an evening.

As I felt myself liking Gunther more than I should, I hoped that wasn't yet another bad life choice. Men had become my blind spot lately. The kryptonite to my Superman... if Superman was a quirky old redhead with arthritis.

But Gunther was just a friend, so it didn't matter, did it? At least that's what I told myself as I adjusted my sunglasses on top of my head and stumbled up Tara's porch steps.

"Rick's missing!" I announced as I swept into Tara's living room, inhaling the strong scent of java.

I wouldn't survive without coffee. Especially this morning.

I shut the front door, leaving the hateful late-morning sun behind me, and headed for the kitchen. Tara was still in her jammies, already pouring a mug of migraine-killing caffeine for me. Gratefully accepting the hot brew, I dropped the scrapbook I had made Rick on her kitchen island and plopped down onto a stool, ready to dish out the latest news to my best friend.

I'd need at least one cup of joe first to get started. I took a sip, mumbling a quick prayer for hangover mercy. But my coffee connoisseur tastebuds detected a subtle blandness. Tara must have noticed my distaste.

"It's decaf," she stated.

No further explanation was needed. My best friend had officially been demoted.

"Decaf?" I whined, unable to grasp the torment Tara was putting me through. "Don't make me slap you silly."

"Calm down, Ginger. It's for the baby." Tara rubbed her belly, which was finally starting to show a baby bump. She was due Christmas day, which was fitting, since it was a very unplanned miracle baby.

"The baby doesn't have a coffee preference," I retorted.

"No caffeine allowed, remember?"

Oh yeah, there were *rules* now about what not to do while pregnant. So many rules. Back when I had babies, car seats were mama's lap, cigarettes were part of every post-partum weight-loss plan, and Spam was on the food pyramid. Now doctors forbid all of those things. How did expectant mothers keep up in this day and age?

"I guess I'll survive," I conceded, dramatically scrunching my face as I took another gulp. "Anywho, did you hear what I said?"

Tara lifted her eyebrows and joined me at the counter. "Yep, Rick is missing. Again. Should I be surprised?"

"It's not the same as before. I mean he actually is missing. As in someone left me this message at the restaurant I was supposed to meet him at last night."

I handed Tara the ad clipping, watching her expression shift from disinterest to curiosity then back to indifference. Then I opened up the scrapbook and pointed out the same date found on the clipping and Studio 54 photo.

"I think someone abducted Rick," I clarified.

"Suuure. Did you check Rick's apartment to see if he's there?"

"I went there last night after leaving the restaurant and he didn't answer the door, and *Large Marge* wasn't in the parking lot."

"*Large Marge*?" Tara looked at me like I was crazy. She gave me that look a lot.

"His motorcycle."

"Oh, well there you have it. His bike is gone, which means he drove away on his own volition," Tara replied, mystery solved.

"But what about this message I got?"

"It didn't occur to you that Rick left this fake threat, hoping to manipulate you into worrying about him while he took off… yet again… like he always does?"

Hm. Okay, I hadn't thought about it that way. But it sounded like an awful lot of effort for Rick to go through just to dupe me. And for what purpose? He never cared enough to jump through these kinds of hoops when he would disappear on me in the past.

Tara seemed to read my doubt, so she bulldozed ahead with her logic.

"For months he's been begging for your forgiveness and asking you to take him back. But he's given you no proof that he's stopped his life of crime. So my guess is that he never really intended to get clean, but he doesn't want to lose you either. Because let's face it, Ging—you're the best thing that ever happened to him. So this," she tapped the clipping with her dirty farm-girl fingernails, "is the perfect ruse to garner your sympathy while he disappears. Then he can return and make up some elaborate lie about where he was—poor, abducted Rick— so that you'll be obligated to take him back."

"You really think he'd go to that extreme, though? I mean, digging up old newspapers in order to send me a very specific message? The 1978 date on this isn't coincidental, Tara. And I just *know* it has something to do with why he's gone."

"I can't interpret the mind or habits of a narcissist, Ginger. But Rick is all about Rick, and his entire history shows it. Don't give him the benefit of the doubt. He hasn't earned it."

Tara made good points, but my gut—as hangover nauseous as it was—told me something bad had happened to him.

"Rick isn't sentimental, Tara. This isn't like him at all."

"He's a pathological liar. And emotionally abusive to you. Don't forget that. And let's say he did get abducted. He made his bed! You can't put yourself at risk by trying to save him. Distance yourself from him, please."

Maybe Tara was right. On more than one occasion I had let my Savior Complex steer me into danger.

I flipped through the scrapbook, just about to close it when a face stopped me short. It was a picture of my oldest son, Benson, whose fifteen-month death anniversary was coming up. I pulled the photograph out of the scrapbook, noticing the tiny circles at the corners where my tears had stained the paper. I hadn't told anyone my little secret, that every month I cried over this picture.

This was the image I had printed for Bennie's funeral, the same one the news station had broadcast when announcing the memorial fund Sloane and I had started.

I recalled taking the picture with mixed emotions. Dressed in an overpriced gray suit that matched the gray in his flashy necklace, Bennie did look charmingly handsome. So handsome I buried him in it so he could look his best when he approached the pearly gates. It was his lucky suit, he once told me. He'd need all the luck he could get to gain entrance into heaven.

He'd bought the Armani virgin wool three-piece—at full price, against my better advice—after he'd been named one of *Bloodson Bay's Most Successful Forty Under Forty*. I hadn't been invited to attend the lavish award ceremony commemorating the town's top forty businessmen. I didn't mind one bit, since my arch-nemesis Colin Roth was hosting it. The leech had stolen my family's beach property inheritance from me; I wasn't going to sit in a room applauding the thieving creatin and his cohorts. Besides, it was too fancy for my humble blood, and spending the night celebrating the rich folks who controlled our town and corrupted our politics wasn't exactly my cup of tea. Sour, just like this decaf coffee.

"You miss him, don't you?" Tara soothed, glancing at Benson's picture.

"Yes, but it's getting a little easier each day," I lied. "I just… I've lost so much and I'd been praying things would be restored between me and Rick. I really thought he had changed. Maybe I don't have the sense God gave a goose."

"Hey, don't say that. You're not dumb. And maybe you're right, that someone is holding Rick against his will. If you want help finding him, I'll go to the police with you and we'll see what they can do, okay?"

I could tell Tara felt bad, and that made me feel good. I wanted her to trust me, that Rick needed my help, because I had a hard time trusting me, too.

"Any ideas on who would want to hurt him?" Tara asked.

Did she have a couple of hours to kill?

"My first guess would be the Valance family. I saw Leonard at the bar right after I got the clipping. That can't be coincidence."

I knew Rick had worked for the corrupt Judge Ewan Valance for decades, running drugs or trafficking people or burying bodies. Who knows what they did under the cover of night?

Judge Valance controlled the town by ensuring criminals stayed on the streets instead of in jail where they belonged. With that same power he had managed to keep himself out of jail after indisputable evidence proved he had done his fair share of crime, which Rick knew about. There's a reason they say the only way two people can keep a secret is if one of them was dead.

"I don't know…" Tara hem-and-hawed. "Considering Judge Valance is currently out on bail, I don't think he'd risk drawing attention to himself like this. Rick is a known associate of the Valances, so would they take a chance by abducting him when they're in the middle of a trial? It's not like Rick was going to talk."

That we knew of.

"I think we should go to the police and report him missing and let them deal with it," Tara added. "It's what anyone would do in a normal missing persons situation."

The only problem was that there was nothing normal about this missing person, or the situation.

Chapter 5

The Bloodson Bay Police Department front desk had just put me on hold for Detective Martina Carillo-Hughes, whom Tara called *Marti* with a familiarity I didn't envy, so I just called her Detective Hughes.

While easy-listening *Muzak* played through the line, Tara's doorbell rang in the background behind me. I wouldn't have given it another thought until I heard Tara say, "Hey, you're here just in time to help with something. Come on in!" just as Detective Hughes picked up the call.

"This is Detective Martina Carillo-Hughes," the detective said coolly.

But Tara's voice carried loudly across the house. "Oh no, what's wrong?"

I didn't like the sound of *that*.

"Uh, hi, Detective…" I mumbled, totally distracted now.

"You've got to be kidding me!" From the living room Tara sounded concerned, and I was dying to know who she was talking to, and about what.

"Hello?" the detective asked the dead air.

"Can you hold on a second?" I spoke into the microphone, my focus completely lost.

"What's this call about?" Annoyance laced the detective's

question.

"Wait until Ginger sees this," I overheard Tara say.

My brain was failing to multitask, and whatever Tara was dealing with felt more urgent.

"Can I call you back?" I asked the detective. "Something just came up."

"Excuse me?" I imagined the detective's shoulder-length curls swaying as she shook her head at me. Martina Carillo-Hughes was as no-nonsense as her ugly BBPD-issued loafers. "You called me, ma'am."

"And… now I've got to hang up," I rushed.

"Is this an emergency?" Detective Hughes' irritation escalated to anger, and I worried she might figure out it was me. Especially with loudmouth Tara mentioning me by name in the background.

"I'm not sure," I answered the detective briefly. "I'll call you back."

"Don't bother," Detective Hughes grumbled. "Unless you have an actual emergency."

"I'm sorry. I gotta go!" I was about to hang up when I heard my name.

"Ginger Mallowan, is this you?" the detective asked. I could tell she already knew the answer.

Oops. Busted.

"Nope!" I yelped in a panic and disconnected the call. I hoped it wasn't a crime to lie to a police officer.

I got up from the island and hurried to the living room, wondering what Tara referred to that I just had to see. Sloane stood in the entryway, sunlight creating a halo around her. She looked put-together as always, except for the hint of a frown wrinkling her flawless face that looked like she wore a perpetual Snapchat beauty filter.

To be young again…

But the girl couldn't cook to save her life.

Sloane was holding a casserole dish I had sent her home with last week when she politely raved about my chicken pot pie. She had been eating *agege* bread and *jollof* rice for over a week, the only two dishes I think she knew how to make after her Nigerian mother gave up trying to teach her. Despite Sloane's protests, I sent her home with potpie leftovers, worried she might otherwise starve.

Using American Sign Language, Sloane signed and mouthed "good morning" as she quickly hugged me hello.

A year and a half ago I had barely enough sign skills to properly sign *I need gas* instead of *I need sex*. I had made that mistake a couple times, in public no less, before Sloane finally corrected my finger placement, the little prankster! But now I could exchange entire conversations without missing a beat. Between Sloane and I teaching Tara, she was quickly catching on, though I still felt the need to interpret when our hands were flying.

"What's going on?" I signed back to Sloane and simultaneously spoke to Tara.

"I stopped by your house to bring back your dish I borrowed last week, and I found this old… newspaper ad taped to your front door. I'm sure it's nothing, but it creeped me out a little."

Another newspaper ad. My heart thumped. My head swirled. I felt lightheaded as the blood drained from my face. And I hadn't even had a *real* cup of coffee yet.

"Are you okay?" Sloane signed.

Was I as pale as I felt?

"This is the second one I've gotten."

"We'll figure it out together, okay?" Sloane offered, patting me on the back.

How did she always manage to remain so calm and collected? I envied her ability to keep her emotions in check, as if nothing could phase her. It made you wonder: Was Sloane born perpetually optimistic, or was she hiding a horrible trauma that hardened her emotions to steel?

Sloane lifted the casserole dish up and carried it to the kitchen with a warm smile. "Do I smell coffee?"

Sloane having a dark past? I chuckled at my own silly notion. Sloane was as ordinary as they came.

"If you could call it that," I signed, following her. "How did you know to find me here?"

Her lip lifted in a half-smirk. "If you're not at home you're usually here. You're pretty predictable."

That was true. I really was... to a fault. Unfortunately, that made me an easy target for whoever was sending these messages.

I took the newspaper clipping from Sloane and gave it a quick look.

"Well, let's see what warning they have for me this time."

Chapter 6

BLOODSON BAY BULLETIN
April 30, 1975

THE BEST THING TO HAPPEN TO YOU SINCE THE RIGHT TO VOTE

Finding yourself bored while your husband is at work? Got too much time on your hands? Throw a Tupperware party for your friends! Forget the lice outbreak at school, and dinner will wait, because this deal you don't want to miss. Join countless other women working from the comfort of your living room. Become a Tupperware hostess today!

Between Sloane's attention to detail, Tara's neat handwriting, and my ability to hold the paper out nice and far, we had figured out what the dire message said in a matter of minutes:

I f you go to p o lice r will d i e

"*If you go to the police, R*—which I assume is Rick—*will die*," Tara deduced pretty easily by the time I had only decoded up to *police*. "So I guess that means we've got to leave Marti out of it."

While I wasn't keen on saving Rick without police protection, I had already figured involving Detective Hughes could be problematic. Especially seeing as Rick was a criminal, and *freeing* him from his captor would most likely end up *imprisoning* him by the system. But at least the message offered two key positives that gave me hope:

The first was that Rick was still alive. Though I doubted Tara would consider that a positive.

The second was that I hadn't technically gone to the police yet. Thankfully I had hung up when I did. So I hadn't screwed up... that I knew of. If the sender was watching me, which it was pretty clear he was—or she was, since I didn't want to assume gender—I couldn't be certain I hadn't done something to make Rick's situation worse.

"What now?" I posed. "I can't go to the police. And the first message told me that if I wanted a future with Rick, I needed to search through the past. But none of these little notes have been helpful in doing that."

"If it's telling you to search through the past, then do just that," Sloane stated plainly, as if she had just solved global hunger.

"That's about as useful as a trap door in a canoe, Sloane. How about offer some ideas on how I do that?"

I was trying to keep my snark in check, I really was, but this game was no fun, and the sender seemed only intent on making a fool of me. I did that to myself quite plenty, thank you very much.

"I think every part of this clipping is a clue. There's a reason he picked this exact date. Do you know of any relevance with it?" Tara asked.

Ah, I knew I kept Tara around for a reason, and why we had jokingly dubbed our trio of crime-solving savvy sleuths *Tara's Angels* instead of *Ginger's Angels*.

"Oh, yeah. April 30, 1975. That day was a biggie, actually. I'll never forget it. Most of the world probably remembers it as the day the Vietnam War ended with the fall of Saigon, but it held a very different significance for me..."

The remembrance came back as fresh as my mam*ó*'s Irish soda bread straight out of the oven. My heart still wore the scars of that spring day. Somehow this sender knew about it, and he scratched at my pain, ripping open the wound all over again.

I pulled a tissue from my sleeve, dotting my eyes as a tear spilled over at the reminiscence. The hem of my shawl caught on my belt—the leather belt Rick had handmade for me as a wedding gift. The craftmanship was incredible, as Rick had quite a gift. Leatherworking was an art to him, evident in the way he cut, stitched, and burnished the belt, then embellished it with rhinestones. He had spent weeks crafting it with me in mind, and I spent years wearing it with him in mind. In fact, I still did...

Suddenly my pants felt too tight, the room too stifling, my skin too hot to wear. I shrugged off my shawl and hung it over the back of the chair.

"Is it warm in here?" I asked, fanning my face. I could feel the flush crawling up my neck.

"I'm actually cold," Tara replied. "But the pregnancy hormones keep giving me alternating cold and hot flashes, so I'm not a good judge of temperature."

Tara grabbed my shawl and wrapped it around her shoulders. "Mind if I borrow this?"

"As long as you don't keep it, you klepto. It's my favorite go-to shawl."

Now that I didn't feel like I would spontaneously combust, my mind returned to April 30, 1975.

"I don't even know where to begin," I said with a sigh.

"What happened, Ginger?" Tara's question was barely above a whisper.

It was supposed to be one of the best days of my life... but it was crushed into one of the single most devastating moments of my life. It was the first time I realized a hard and undeniable truth that I would spend a lifetime trying—and failing—to deny:

That I would die for the man I loved.

Chapter 7

April 30, 1975

The local news had just announced the end of the Vietnam War. Soldiers were coming home, but not my Rick, because he had never left. Instead, he had managed to dodge the draft, and I had been unpatriotically relieved about it. I should have felt ashamed that other women's husbands surrendered their lives while mine stayed safe on American soil. What did that say about Rick, putting himself before his country? What did that say about me, that I was secretly glad for it?

But the end of the war wasn't at the top of my mind tonight. Nor was the fishy scent of salmon loaf that filled the kitchen while I picked out my rear-huggin' husband-approved hot pants and a smock top with wedge-heeled espadrilles. I had plans to make it extra special for tonight's main event:

It was April 30, 1975, our one-year anniversary.

My gift to Rick was salmon loaf and love-making. Rick's gift to me was a road trip to Missouri to watch a tractor-pull event starring the infamous *Bigfoot* monster truck. I knew it was weird to prefer watching *Bigfoot* over Broadway, but what can I say? I was a small-town country girl with small-town country tastes. Despite Rick's insistence that no one but me wanted to see a big truck lug a tractor, I believed this was the start of something big… pun intended.

When a co-worker first told me about the monstrous Ford F-250 that had been outfitted with ginormous wheels and a supercharged engine that could tow anything while crushing everything in its path, I was smitten. I just *had* to see it for myself.

Rick had been baffled by my obsession, but he loved me enough to find out when the next tractor pull in the Show-Me State was and book a motel. As luck would have it, it was the weekend following our anniversary, and we were set to leave after dinner. I made one of Rick's favorite meals to show him how much I appreciated him making my monster-truck dream come true.

The phone rang just as I finished setting a candlelight table for two. I ran to the television to turn down the sound of Louise Jefferson fussin' at George, then yanked the olive-colored receiver off the base, huffing as I answered.

"Hello?" I greeted.

"Heyyy… how's my stone fox tonight?" Rick's voice sounded tentative, like he was covering up bad news with a cheesy compliment.

I had a feeling I knew why he was calling, but not tonight. Any night but tonight.

"Dinner's almost on the table, Casanova, and it smells amazing," I lied. Fish never smelled amazing. "It should be hot and ready right when you get home—just like me," I teased, trying to add levity to a bad situation I felt brewing.

"About that…" He drifted off, and I knew it.

Rick wasn't going to make it. I would have given him the hairy eyeball if he was in the same room. My hands began to tremble with a growing rage. My mood ring darkened to black, along with my state of mind.

"No, don't you dare cancel on me tonight, Rick Mallowan! It's our one-year anniversary, and by God I *will* get priority over your good-for-nothing, jive-turkey boss."

"Gingersnap, that good-for-nothing boss pays the bills."

"Pays the bills, huh? Where's all the overtime pay for staying late all these nights? Your boss is so cheap he wouldn't give a nickel to see Jesus ridin' a bicycle."

"That's because I'm working my way up, babe," Rick pleaded. "Good things are coming, I swear. He's given me more responsibility."

"You already have a responsibility, Rick. To me, your wife."

"But this is different. I'm tired of being a nobody who doesn't deserve you. With this new opportunity I can be somebody!"

Rick failed to appreciate the fact that he already was somebody—to me. When had that no longer been enough?

"What kind of opportunity are you talking about, anyways?" I asked, genuinely curious. I wasn't against moving up in the world, but not any cost.

"A shot at making your dreams come true. If things work out, I'll buy you the biggest house in Bloodson Bay, with a cute barn for a horse you've wanted since you were a little girl. You'll be the envy of the town."

"I don't want to be the envy of the town, and I don't need any of those things, Rick. I just want *you*."

"Don't you get it?" Rick's voice hardened, as if he could force his point across the phone cord, into my ear, and push it into my heart. But my heart was already full; I didn't want anything more than what I had. "We could be *rich*, Gingersnap."

"Rich?" I laughed. "The only way folks like us get rich is illegally. It's not illegal, is it?"

I meant the question as a joke, but the hesitation in Rick's reply would keep me up late that night with worry scrambling my brain.

"Uh, of course not," he finally said. "You know, it hurts that my boss believes in me, the guys at work believe in me, but my own wife don't."

"Sometimes I think that when the Lord was handin' out brains, you thought God said *trains* and passed 'cause you don't like to travel. Don't you see you don't matter to them?"

It was easy for his "colleagues"—or let's just call them the *criminals* that they were—to believe in a man they could use and dispose of. They didn't care about him; they were using him. But I could never get Rick to see that. And even if I could, it would kill his pride to find out the truth.

"This is important, Ging. I wish you could get over yourself and support me."

"Okay, then tell me: What could possibly be more important than our one-year anniversary tonight?"

Rick never did answer me as he sputtered an apology and hung up. That night, as Rick annihilated our anniversary, I showed up at his mechanic shop.

He wasn't there, but his co-worker was… with a warning to go home and forget about Rick if I knew what was good for me. Of course I didn't know what was good for me; I willingly chose to stay with him, didn't I?

Our one-year anniversary forced me to face a hard truth: I

was no longer the most important person in my husband's life. I had been replaced… but it would take years for me to unravel what exactly had replaced me, and just how dangerous it was, until it nearly killed me.

Chapter 8

I had gotten enough pity from Tara and Sloane to fill a horse trough. After telling them my woeful tale of Rick's Anniversary Annihilation—my nickname for the event that would change the course of our future after I realized my husband was stepping deep into something that smelled illegal—we exchanged the coffee and toast for cabernet and tissues. But even after venting, I still felt like a bottled-up soda, shaken and ready to burst. I needed advice that wasn't biased against Rick, and there was only one place to find it.

Alone.

After I left Tara with a hug, and forced a frozen tuna casserole on Sloane, I wandered around my empty house. Then I headed right back out the door and decided to go for a drive where I could hear my thoughts. And feel my worry.

For the next couple hours I drove while I worried, past the Loving Arms Children's Home where on the court outside the main house, a group of boys got schooled by a petite gal in a rowdy game of basketball. Underdogs winning always cheered me up… especially when they were girls.

I followed a familiar route to Debbie's Diner, although the salt-weary sign above the 1950's-style building read *Debbie's Die* after the "n" and "r" in *Diner* had burned out. Recognizing most of the vehicles in the parking lot, I kept going, not in the mood for polite hellos.

Passing empty beach access roads that tourists usually overran during the summer, I bumped along the broken highway and turned around in a forlorn shopping plaza where Nails by Nellie was the only remaining business next to a vacant Blockbuster video store.

Eventually I reached the outskirts of the town limits, where the So-so Southern Motel sat under a cluster of live oaks. There I noticed married Mr. Goodly's truck parked outside of Room 6 next to also-married Mrs. McNaught's minivan.

Tsk, tsk. There was nothing *good* about this *mcnaughty* meetup, I chuckled to myself. Wait until the girls heard about this! Sunday's sermon about gossiping pricked my conscious just then, and I *checked myself before I wrecked myself* and kept driving.

The horizon was a dusty gray by the time I arrived at the one place you never visit after dark. From time immemorial, horror movies warned about it, Stephen King traumatized us over it, and campfire ghost stories scared us away from it. But it was the only place I could turn to:

Benson's gravesite.

The Bloodson Bay Cemetery would have fit perfectly into one of those horror movies or Stephen King novels or ghost stories. The creaking rusted front gate, the ancient crumbling gravestones, the overgrown eerie isolation… it was the stuff of nightmares. But it was also the only place I could unload my secrets with only the judgement of the dead to condemn me. And considering they were all probably dealing with their own judgement, I doubted they cared much about mine.

The afternoon sun was long gone by the time I found Bennie's modest headstone using the weak flashlight beam from my phone. The crooked slab of marble in front of a loose pile of dirt was all I had to remember my firstborn by—along with the donation box still sitting in my trunk.

I came here often to revisit old, sweet memories, usually choosing to remember him as the little boy with kissable chubby cheeks. Now that Bennie was hovering somewhere in the cosmos, he always listened respectfully to my feelings and opinions, a sad reality I wish I could have enjoyed more during his life on earth. But I would take what I could get, even if the only listening ears were the owl's, who kept hooting at me from the distant wood line as I spoke.

"I miss you, Bennie," I began.

Hoot hoot, the owl echoed thoughtfully.

"I don't know how to help your dad. You'd probably know what thug to extort, or what crime boss to blackmail. Tara and Sloane think I should just leave it alone, but I can't. It's complicated. As I'm sure you already know."

The owl hooted again in understanding.

"Please give me some kind of sign, or advice, or something. I'm afraid I'm going to screw up and cost your dad his life."

I sighed and sat down in the mud, rambling away to a piece of rock.

"I've asked God what to do, but I feel like He's put me on hold. I can't go to the police, and Tara's not keen on helping me."

Her pregnancy tuckered her out enough as it was. On top of that, her husband Chris was on a job hunt as the financial burden grew more precarious by the day. Not to mention her daughter

Nora was out of town homeschooling with her other grandma while applying to colleges… Tara certainly didn't need any added stress. Especially not the missing-person mystery-solving kind.

"There's no way I'm dragging Sloane into it, as she's busy enough as it is."

With the memorial fund to handle, and running her business Feel the Noize Party Planning, my insta-famous friend had her hands overflowing with celebrity parties to plan. It was a wonder Sloane wanted to live in Bloodson Bay when superstars from Los Angeles to New York City threw thousands of dollars at her feet just to plan their kids' sweet sixteen parties featuring extravagant circus themes or live performances from Snoop Dogg. I was lucky to get Rod Stewart's *Every Picture Tells a Story* record album for my sixteenth birthday just so I could listen to "Maggie May" on an endless loop.

I had been devastated when Rick cracked my precious album in half over his knee during a particularly bad fight. It had been one of my most prized possessions, a rare and extravagant gift from my poverty-stricken parents when I was growing up. Ten minutes after Rick destroyed it I forgave him as he wept at my feet and promised to buy me a new one.

He never did.

"The fact is, if your dad's disappearance has something to do with his criminal enemies, maybe it's best I not get involved at all. But I love him, Bennie. I really do. Even after everything he's done…"

And that's where I kept ending up. The same full circle that got me nowhere.

A coastal chill saturated the damp air, sending shivers up

my body. I stood up, wiping the sandy dirt off my pants when it occurred to me that I was standing on… well, dirt. Not grass, like the grave had been last month, and the month before that, and the month before that.

I stepped back and visually traced the large rectangular patch of freshly turned-up earth. Where was my son's spongy green hill? Where were the canna lilies I had planted around his tombstone?

I glanced around to see if any other gravesites had been disturbed. It was as if someone had dug up Bennie's coffin. And *only* Bennie's coffin.

Skimming the surrounding area with my light, tire tracks chewed into the earth where I was standing. Two truck-width trails bent the grass, thick treads imprinting the ground, leading down to the cemetery exit.

The grass hadn't yet popped upright. Which meant this was recent.

At the base of Bennie's gravestone was the dried-up bouquet of flowers I had brought last month, now drawing my attention to the stone. It sat askew, as if it had been knocked sideways while some necromancing weirdo unearthed my son's gravesite.

A new chill popped goosebumps across my flesh.

Why the h-e-double hockey sticks would someone want to dig up my son's grave?

Chapter 9

Debbie's Diner was packed full, from the peeling red pleather booths to every chrome barstool at the L-shaped counter. Sitting at our usual table by the window, I stared through the grease-smudged glass toward the bay. Along the beach, strobes of light streaked across the gray as children with flashlights searched for ghost crabs in the sand.

A slight movement shifted my view through the glass, revealing my disheveled reflection. I nearly startled at my auburn hair mushroomed in a state of lawless anarchy.

The kitchen buzzed with waitresses calling orders, and the checker-floored dining room hummed with the energy of gossiping patrons. When it was suppertime on a Friday night, the whole town showed up for Debbie's shrimp 'n' grits.

I wasn't here for the food, though, no matter how tempting it smelled. I was doing the serving tonight, and the main dish was a heap of a predicament.

"I don't even know what to think," Tara confessed after I'd told them how I found Bennie's tampered-with tomb.

While Tara and Sloane cleaned their plates of grits smothered in a lemon cream sauce, I stared at my pile of loaded cheese fries, my appetite nonexistent. (Hard to believe anything could make me turn down Debbie's fries.)

"What did the groundskeeper say about it?" Sloane signed.

"He was useless," I signed back.

After making half a dozen calls tracking down the cemetery groundskeeper, Joe, he proved to be no help at all. When he finally met me at the graveyard entrance, I knew why he had gotten the job. Smelling like a rotting corpse himself, he probably felt a kinship with all the deceased. He was right at home.

Needless to say, Groundskeeper Joe hadn't ordered any digging, didn't have any burials on the books, and he didn't even know it was illegal to dig up a grave. (It was indeed illegal without formal authorization—I checked.) Since there were no cameras on the property or anywhere in proximity to it, there was no way to find out who had done it unless a witness came forward.

So of course Groundskeeper Joe contacted the BBPD to let them know, which was exactly what I *didn't* want to happen… just in case this had something to do with Rick. After all, I couldn't overlook the timing of it. Coincidence? I think not. It wasn't every day a dead body got unearthed in Bloodson Bay… though I had to admit it was happening more often than not lately.

Adding worry on top of my uneasiness, now I feared whoever held Rick captive would think I was the one who went to the police, despite their warnings.

"I still can't wrap my brain around why someone would dig up a corpse," Sloane added.

"There had to have been something in Benson's casket that they wanted, I'm assuming. Any idea what that could be?" Tara asked.

"Is an Armani suit worth that much?" I asked.

"Not unless it was made from the Shroud of Turin."

I cocked my head, confused.

Tara rolled her eyes and chuckled. "You know, the cloth artifact they say has the face of Jesus on it?"

At my age you unknowingly curated what information your brain held on to, and mine didn't retain much beyond my soap operas and my latest meal (even then, I usually couldn't recall *if* I ate, let alone *what* I ate).

"Speaking of sweet baby Jesus, I feel the anti-Christ's presence in our midst." I gestured toward the end of our wall where Judge Ewan Valance sat at a corner booth with his cronies, while random diners waited to greet him with handshakes and hugs. My guess was he paid them off to publicly inflate his ego.

Judge Valance became a gosh-darn celebrity after the newspapers circulated the story of his son Victor's *unexpected murder* (yeah right—anyone with sense knew the slimeball was on half a dozen hit lists). Judge Valance became sympathetic victim.

On top of that, the media buried the story of the Judge's involvement in Sloane's mother Alika's abduction decades ago. Like the terrible father he was, he threw all the blame on his dead son once audiotape evidence of the crime came to light— how convenient. That case had only recently been exposed, and we hoped Alika Apara's witness testimony would put the Judge behind bars where he belonged.

"I can't believe he has the gall to show his face in public after what he did to my mother," Sloane seethed. "How is he even out on bond? He abducted her and held her in a bunker!

How much more psycho can you get?"

"When you're rich enough, you can get away with anything," Tara signed.

"All of those people greet him like he's God's gift to Bloodson Bay. They should know what he did, what kind of scumbag he really is. I wouldn't be surprised if he's behind Rick's disappearance." I stood up, the booth's torn leather catching on my pant leg. "Maybe I'll ask him." I wasn't afraid to confront the devil head-on.

Sloane watched me with a placid poise.

"Sit your rear back down," Tara insisted, yanking me into my seat. "Now is *not* the time or place to deal with him, Ging."

"My husband is missing, and my son's grave has been messed with. I'd bet the farm that man," I shot a glare down the aisle, "has something to do with it. Besides, it's not like talking to him could make things any worse than they already are."

Why yes, yes it could.

And Judge Ewan Valance was about to prove that very fact as he sauntered up to our booth with a crap-eatin' grin on his face that made my palm twitch with an urge to slap it right off.

"I didn't know they let criminals out of jail for supper," I commented snarkily.

"Innocent until proven guilty in a court of law, my dear," he said snidely. "I would know. I'm a judge, after all."

As if any of us needed the reminder that he somehow held on to his title, despite being under investigation for kidnapping charges.

"A corrupt one."

"Prove it, then." He stood there, glaring down at me, daring me to face off with him. "But I would think you have more important things to deal with than picking a fight with me, Ginger Mallowan."

"What's that supposed to mean?" I asked.

"I'm just saying that you should get your own house in order before you start trying to tear mine down."

"Are you threatening my friend?" Tara interjected.

"Is *now* the time and place to deal with him?" I muttered to Tara under my breath.

Judge Valance slammed his palms on the table, then leaned over until his face was inches from Tara's.

"If you know what's good for you, you'll mind your own business. You've got a husband out of work, don't you?" His gaze traveled down to her belly. "And clearly a bun in the oven. It'd be a shame if you lost everything all because you don't know your place."

All this time Sloane silently observed, her eyes flicking back and forth as she followed the interaction. When she slowly rose to her feet, jaw set, eyes stony, lips tight, I would have feared her if I didn't know she was on my side.

She slid out of the booth and stood before the Judge, eye-to-eye with him at her willowy height, boldly staring him down.

"Do you have something to say?" He sneered. "Oh, that's right. You can't speak."

"Oh, I don't need to speak in order to kill you," Sloane signed.

The room temperature seemed to drop as I felt a coldness surround her, spreading as if filling every empty space around us. The Judge didn't know what she had said, that much was clear in his condescending but confused expression. But I felt the threat's vibrations crawl up my skin, slip inside me, claiming me against my will. Was Sloane actually capable of killing a man? Right here, right now… I actually thought she could.

Without another word the Judge straightened his back, his nose so high in the air he could drown in a rainstorm. Then he turned to leave. He took a step, paused, and glanced back at Tara.

"Oh, and since your husband is looking for a job, I'm always hiring. I'm sure I could find some menial labor he could do."

Like digging up graves? I wondered.

"Over my dead body," Tara spat back.

"Well, that can be arranged," the Judge said with a wry smile. Then he swept out of the diner with a cocky gait, leaving me clammy and breathless, Tara bewildered and fuming, and Sloane… well, if looks could kill… he'd be a dead man.

"He knows about Rick," I whispered.

"Are you sure that's what he was referring to?" Tara asked.

"What else would he be talking about? Besides, he's the most likely one behind it. He has to be the one who's holding him."

"I dunno, Ging." I knew Tara was skeptical that he'd do anything to draw more attention to himself when he was prepping for the court case of his life. "He's got eyes and ears all over town. There's no telling what he knows. That doesn't mean he did it."

The waitress returned, standing where Judge Valance had been moments before, dropping a black plastic check tray on the table. Clipped to it was a single check. Tara picked it up and examined it.

"Penny, can you split the bill three ways?" Tara asked.

"Oh, honey, you're all set. Someone came in and paid the bill for ya'll."

"Wait, what?" While I was grateful for the free meal, I learned the hard way that everything came with a price.

"Yep, even the tip was covered," Penny added. "This is your receipt."

I yanked the tray from Tara, reading the receipt on top. Sure enough, our supper was paid in full—along with a generous tip. But that wasn't the weirdest part. Clipped underneath the check was an envelope. Unmarked.

No, it couldn't be.

"Oh, I didn't notice that under there," Penny said. "She must have slipped it under the receipt."

I opened the flap and peeked inside. Of course it would be another disturbing addition to my life-or-death scavenger hunt of morbidly cryptic clippings.

"Tara, Sloane, look." I held out the opened envelope so they could see inside.

"Who paid for our meal?" Tara asked the waitress. "You said a *she*?"

"Yep," Penny confirmed. "Some blonde gal. I didn't get a good look at her, though. It's been a night."

"Did she pay with a debit card?" I hoped Penny wouldn't mind breaking a rule or two by letting me take a peek at the name on the credit card used.

"Nope, cash." Of course it wouldn't be so simple to get a name. "Maybe you got a secret admirer, Ginger," Penny said with a wink. "But I gotta go. Tables don't wait themselves!"

While Penny rushed off, I dreaded what mysterious message the sender had that was so urgent I couldn't even get through a meal without being bothered.

"Three notes in two days," Sloane deduced. "It seems like your sender is amping up for something big."

Yes, it was heating up pretty quickly and I was just as clueless now over what the sender wanted from me as I was two days ago.

Chapter 10

BLOODSON BAY BULLETIN
August 16, 1977

LET YOUR PERSONALITY BE THE REASON NO ONE WANTS TO VISIT YOUR HOUSE…

…not your overcrowded stuff! Your living space is scarier than President Carter's oil crisis. Clean up your rooms, and your life, by storing your belongings at Stow Away, Don't Throw Away Storage now!

"I have to admit, I like the marketing." Tara read the newspaper clipping aloud with a chuckle.

"What do you make of it?" Sloane signed. "Does the date mean anything to you, Ginger?"

"None that I recall."

I could barely remember last week let alone last year. I wasn't sure how this person—shockingly a blonde woman, I discovered—could expect me to pull decades-old dates and their personal significance out of my sleeve like I was a magician.

How was I to know what happened on a random August day in 1977?

"Let's start by figuring out the message," Tara suggested.

Sloane glanced at the paper. "Fourteen," she signed.

"Huh? Fourteen what?" I asked.

"That's the message. Fourteen." Sloane shrugged, and Tara looked just as nonplussed.

Okay, now that was useless. How was a random number supposed to help me figure out these supposed clues that weren't clueing me in to how to save my husband?

"Fourteen? What kind of message is that?" I whined. "Fourteen days before Rick is killed? Fourteen hours until a building blows up? Bring fourteen dollars in ransom money to the storage unit? I'm done!" I yelled, smacking my hand down on the table and stepping out of the booth.

Tara and Sloane sat in stunned silence, watching me slam the table three more times: "Done! Done! Done!"

I was too old and tired to play this stupid game over a man I wasn't even sure I wanted to save. Right now I should have been enjoying my golden years sipping margaritas on a Caribbean beach, not sleuthing around Bloodson Bay following potential murder leads that led me nowhere but to an early grave.

Grabbing my purse, I heaved it up onto my shoulder and stomped through the diner to the door, letting it slam shut behind me in a frantic jingle. I finally calmed down a beat after the cold night air hit me while I paced the sidewalk and the ocean sounds mollified my madness.

Another jingle, then a hand rested warmly on my shoulder.

"I think you figured it out, Ging," a whisper came behind

me.

I turned to find Tara and Sloane.

"What do you mean?"

"You mentioned the storage unit. I think that's where we're supposed to go," Tara explained. "I looked up Stow Away, Don't Throw Away Storage on Google Maps, and while it's no longer in operation, the old building is still there, according to the pictures. If there's a unit number fourteen, that's probably where this is leading us."

"It's a couple blocks away from Loving Arms Children's Home," Sloane added. "We could be there in ten minutes."

"Speaking of which," Tara switched subjects, "Sloane, don't forget I'm meeting at your house tomorrow around eight o'clock, after I pick Chris up from the airport. Again, thanks so much for offering to plan the fall festival for the kids."

Sloane's innovative party planning was what had made her semi-famous to the point where Feel the Noize Party Planning put Bloodson Bay on the map. That, and our high body count ratio per capita.

With a heart of gold, Sloane gave Tara the friends and family discount for the children's home... which ended up being free. There was no better deal than a big-hearted friend.

A clatter echoed from the alley behind the diner.

"Ladies, I think someone's lurking back there." I stepped toward the sound, but Tara's hand on my shoulder stopped me.

"Don't, Ginger. It's probably a cat or something. Let's just get going."

A sound of shoes smacking pavement, then a closing car door followed, but I couldn't pull a form from the shifting shadows.

"Since when do cats drive cars?" I asked.

"It's getting late, and my feet are swelling more by the minute," Tara whined. "Are we going to Stow Away, Don't Throw Away or not?"

I had thought I could break away from this, from Rick, but maybe I was chained for life to his iron ball. (Get your mind out of the gutter!)

Fifteen minutes later we were pulling up to the gate that encircled the Stow Away, Don't Throw Away Storage property. I sang and bobbed along to Elvis Presley's "Hound Dog" playing on the radio, which jogged a memory that I couldn't quite latch on to.

During the early seventies I had compared Rick to the King of Rock and Roll—Elvis's early years, I made sure to add. Rick didn't like the comparison to the later years when the King began to look and sound like the sad dog he sang about. No thanks to his drug habit, he had become all hat and no cattle.

It had made big news the day Elvis was found dead in his Graceland mansion. On the toilet, too. What a way to go. A legend, gone forever. Hearing the song evoked perfect recall of that day.

It had been hotter than Satan's house cat that August afternoon. I was at a rodeo with Rick, nursing his broken nose and cracked cheekbone with my precious cup of ice after he'd picked a fight with the wrong cowboy. Rick ended up signing over the title to the motorcycle he called *Rhinestone Cowboy*— the bike that pre-dated *Large Marge*—named after our cowboy and damsel in distress bedroom role-play where I played Dolly Parton and he played my Rhinestone Cowboy. Anything to keep the spark in our marriage!

It was a night of tears as Elvis's death announcement circled the rodeo crowd and Rick parted with his beloved bike. Everyone went wild with speculation after the news broke out, women cryin' into their beers and men consoling their cryin' women. And me cryin' over my blistered toes as we ended up hitchhiking home that night.

"Oh my gosh, I remember now!" I exclaimed out of the blue as we parked the car along the road. "Elvis!"

"Uhhh, yeah, that's Elvis on the radio," Tara said.

"No, the date. August 16, 1977. That's the day Elvis died," I explained, but Tara looked even more confused than before.

"What's Elvis have to do with Rick?"

"That same day we were at a rodeo when Rick got in a huge fight with some bull rider. The guy almost put Rick in the hospital, like it was personal."

At the time, I couldn't understand why my peace-and-love husband would pick a fight with a guy who handled angry bulls for a living, but Rick never said a word after he found me at the concessions, his face beaten to a pulp, letting me know we'd be hitchhiking home.

"But now it makes sense. The only way Rick would have parted with *Rhinestone Cowboy* was if he owed the guy money."

I knew I probably made no sense to Tara or Sloane as I pieced together my random thoughts, but it didn't matter. I had the clue I was searching for.

"The bike—that's the key!" I shouted.

"Oh, I'm picking up what you're putting down," Tara said. "If we can find out who Rick signed his motorcycle title over to, it *might* lead us to whoever is behind this. *If* it's even connected."

Tara's sarcasm wasn't lost on me. Obviously she wasn't picking up what I was putting down at all.

"Look, the clues are supposed to make me '*search the past*,' right?" I reminded her. "I'm searching, and this is what I'm finding."

"It can't hurt to dig into it. How do you find an old motorcycle title?" Sloane asked.

"Ya'll are the internet gurus, not me," I said with a shrug. "But first things first. We've got a rusty old storage unit to search. I hope everyone has their tetanus shots!"

Chapter 11

August 16, 1977

John Wayne was the reason I was stuck on the back of the *Rhinestone Cowboy* motorcycle, in the brutal August heat, watching the tops of my fair-skinned thighs burn to a crisp.

I had never been to a real live rodeo before today, and as sweat dripped down my forehead, soaking strands of red hair to my brow while the rest tangled in the wind, I wasn't sure I even cared to watch a bull get yanked around by his balls. But Rick, obsessed with all things Wild West while stuck in a North Carolina beach town, felt like maybe if he was in proximity to a real cowboy, some of it might rub off on him. And so we went.

The ride to the grounds where the rodeo was being held was long and winding… and did I mention hot? Eventually I whined enough for Rick to take a detour to grab a cold Tab soda.

After a miserable thirty more minutes, we rode into the small town of Rothsville to stop for $0.62 per gallon gas and a $0.25 Tab—plus the 10-cent bottle deposit—that I drank in less than a minute.

The gas station attendant approached me hiding under the shade of the awning. A cigarette bobbed on the end of his lips while he clutched a beer can. It explained his brown rambling teeth and liver-failing sallow eyes.

"Not every day I meet a pretty gal like you." He sidled next to me, eyeing me with roving gaze that made my skin itch.

I nodded with a stiff grin.

He gestured across the street to a used car lot full of junk cars and one shiny new electric blue Cadillac Eldorado that made no sense in this town.

"Check out that beauty," he commented. "Custom paint job, too."

It wasn't a monster truck, so it didn't impress me much.

"That there car belongs to the town's owner. Friend of mine."

I think that was intended to woo me, but it only made me want to run away faster. One look down the street and I could guess who it was. Along the destitute blocks of empty storefronts, Corbin Roth Real Estate signs sprung up touting his growing ownership of the town. His name was printed in gold text against a red background. It was the opposite of patriotic in the 1970s, considering the Cold War still raged on and his signs looked like USSR endorsements.

Rumors circulated in my neighborhood about Roth's ruthless schemes to drive us beachfront residents out of Bloodson Bay so he could develop high-rise condominiums, which were becoming all the rage these days. Roth's first mistake was thinking the locals could be so easily bought. His second mistake was assuming anyone would want to vacation in Bloodson Bay.

"Anyone who's a friend of Corbin Roth's is an enemy of mine," I stated, looking the old man square in the eyes.

He hmphed. "I ain't said we're *best* friends. I just... know him. Why you hate him so bad?"

"*Rothsville*?" I mocked. "He's too big for his britches, ain't he? What a scumbag," I muttered.

"A *rich* scumbag," the gas station attendant added. I couldn't tell if it was envy or admiration in his tone.

Rick had finished topping off the gas tank and joined us in the shade. "Who's a rich scumbag?"

"Corbin Roth. You think it's coincidence this town has his name plastered all over every bench and block and it's named Rothsville? Can you get more egocentric than that?"

"If he's willing to put money into rebuilding the town and buying up the vacant buildings, there's no harm in naming it after himself. I'm pretty sure just about every town is named after someone."

"It's arrogant, if you ask me. He's a greedy, self-serving, lying, manipulative snake. Did you know he tricked Mrs. Downer into selling her house way under market value? If he's not above stealing from old ladies, I can't imagine what else he'd do to earn a buck."

"Better watch what you say. There's ears and eyes in these parts." The crease between the gas station attendant's eyebrows puckered up with concern.

I flicked off the sky. "Then I hope he sees this!"

"Ging, stop. You don't understand because you're not a businessman," Rick came to Corbin Roth's defense. "You can't blame a guy for earning a living."

"Even if he does so through corruption and lying?" I spat back.

"Take a chill pill. That's just hearsay. Maybe Mrs. Downer should read the fine print next time."

It almost sounded as if Rick *admired* the sleazeball!

I wasn't going to argue with Rick over the virtues Corbin Roth clearly lacked, a creep whose name didn't deserve to be uttered by my cherry red lips.

"Whatever, Rick. If you ever become like him, I'll leave you faster than a one-legged man in a butt-kickin' competition."

Back on the road—and under the merciless sun—we were maybe a mile or two down from Rothsville when I saw the most amazing thing.

"Look!" I yelled into Rick's ear over the sound of gushing air. Gripping his waist with one arm, I carefully released him with the other arm and pointed.

Rick slowed to a stop on the side of the road and let me gawk at the most beautiful creature I'd ever seen. A beige draft horse.

"Ain't she something?" I said wistfully, dismounting the bike and walking to the split-rail fence. I hopped up on the rail, straddling it to get a closer look.

Now, to many that might sound like a silly childlike obsession, to ogle an everyday horse. But this was no ordinary horse. It was an American cream draft horse, one of only 200 left in existence, most of which lived up in Williamsburg, Virginia, a few hours north of us.

Ever since my parents took me as a little girl to see the wild horses running along the beaches of Ocracoke Island, I'd dreamed of one day owning my own horse. I would have gladly taken any gelding or mare that needed a home, but an American cream draft… that was my pretty pipe dream.

"You want that horse?" Rick joined me at the rail, staring at me, as if seriously considering buying her for me. "I'll get her for you."

"Ha, close the shades! That's an American cream draft horse. She's gotta be worth thousands, Rick. She's a rare breed. Pretty to look at, but too rich for my blood."

He wrapped his arms around me from behind, holding me close.

"Whatever you set your heart to, I'm gonna give you one day. If an American cream draft horse is what you want, then an American cream draft horse is what you'll get. Because I love you more than anything, Gingersnap."

It was dangerously easy to be consumed by Rick's wild but loyal heart. Speaking with such earnestness, his sincerity nearly made me cry. I was the only one he showed his vulnerability to, which made me the only one who knew it for what it truly was: a grip so tight it hurt.

"And I'll do *anything* to prove it to you."

Chapter 12

We had almost passed by the iron gate to Stow Away, Don't Throw Away Storage, which had been eaten away by years of salty air and neglect. Only one streetlight illuminated the entire block, and the moonless sky was of little help tonight. While a padlocked chain held the fence closed, it didn't take more than nimble maneuvering to slip through the crooked opening.

I wiped orange rust off of my hands onto my pants while scanning the long, narrow building. The stretch of white brick was interrupted by evenly placed sun-bleached turquoise garage doors. I counted the number of doors in the single row: fifteen.

Finally something was going my way!

I was ready to get some answers. Apparently so was Sloane as she led the charge. We were off like a herd of turtles, moving carefully along the building to avoid being seen. Not that anyone would have been lurking in these parts of Bloodson Bay, where even the vermin knew better than to be out past dark. I had to be clandestine, just in case someone was watching me.

Sloane turned on her flashlight and headed toward the furthest end, where storage unit fourteen would most likely be. Reaching the second to last unit, she shone the white beam along the bottom and sides of the door, finding a metal handle next to a number plate: 14.

The staple hasp hardware where a padlock would have secured the door was intact but held no lock, thank God.

Another thing coming up Ginger!

Although the door took some tough love to roll upward, the three of us combined managed to heave it open just above our shoulders, where its eroded joints finally resisted our efforts and firmly stuck. Each of us lit up our phone lights, the beams pouring over the cluttered space like water, filling the shadows with light.

A burnt orange Eames chair sat in front of a hideous rattan wicker desk shoved against the wall, drawers open with contents littered on every surface area. A pet rock held a stack of papers down next to a dusty Atari game console. A lampshade sat upside-down in the far corner, the glass base a shattered mess of shards.

"It looks like someone was already here," Tara commented as she wandered around the room, poking around at random.

"This stuff is all so *old*," Sloane signed, picking up a yellow 8-track player that brought back my nostalgia.

I recalled toggling from program to program on my own 8-track tapes once upon a time.

"The 1970s aren't *that* old," I grumbled, the adrenaline of late-night sleuthing pumping through me with a youthful vigor I rather enjoyed.

Making my way along the closest wall, I stepped in something wet. A dark puddle splashed under my Easy Spirit shoes.

"Ladies, I think I found blood!" I yelped, teetering back.

Tara joined behind me, examining it closely with her flashlight. "No, that looks like motor oil."

False alarm. But if it was motor oil, had *Large Marge* and her leaky oil pan been in here?

Sloane squealed as she walked headfirst into a cobweb. Swiping frantically around her, it was the first time she showed any sign of fright since this whole thing started. Facing off with a bloodthirsty judge didn't bother her, but a silky spidery thread sent her running? I would never understand some people...

"Scared?" I teased Sloane.

"Of psychopaths? No. Of spiders? Yes!"

Tara picked up a stack of papers that had been tossed on a dresser, leafing through them. "What do you think your secret admirer is searching for?"

I wasn't sure *secret admirer* was the right description for my news clippings courier, but at long as it didn't turn into *Fatal Attraction*, I'd accept it.

"This all looks like accounting records." Tara's attention was fixed on a handful of documents as she spoke. "And all of it is in Rick's name."

"So this was *his* storage unit? I had assumed it was his abductor's. I guess Rick had more secrets up his sleeve than I realized."

While Sloane continued picking through junk and Tara continued shuffling through papers, I reached the back of the unit and stopped short with a little gasp.

The most alarming thing I noticed wasn't the large metal filing cabinet with drawers jutting out. Or the mess of papers scattered over the floor. Or the broken glass crunching underfoot.

A chill ran up my spine.

"Guys... you need to see this..."

It was a metal folding chair that yanked my attention. Specifically what was at the feet of the chair. A shallow pool of something dark and liquid, at one point. This time it *definitely* looked like blood. And something else, equally disturbing. I knelt down to get a better look, examining four cut zip ties lying on the concrete floor.

"I think someone was held against their will here," I said, picking up one of the snapped zip ties and holding it over my head to show them. I dabbed my finger at the dark droplets on the floor. It wasn't fresh enough to be wet, but not fully dry either. A sticky in-between.

"And this time I actually did find blood. I think it was recent."

Across the dim room, Sloane signed something, but her fingers were obscured by shadows. I couldn't read what she was telling me, but her movements looked urgent.

"How much blood are we talking about?" Tara asked as she wound through the clutter toward me.

"Enough," I stated.

"That can't be good." Bringing a handful of papers with her, Tara stopped where I stooped, staring at the blood. "Maybe they just moved him? It's not really that much blood. He could be alive, Ging." Tara's warbled voice indicated she was being generous with the optimism.

She dropped the handful of papers at my knees and hugged me. For a moment I wanted to sink into her arms and cry, but then I noticed something else. A word popping out at me from one of the papers she had set down.

"What is this?" I asked, picking through the papers until I found the one in question.

"I don't know. I just grabbed a handful and started reading."

"This is recent," I said, pointing out the date at the top.

April 30, 2019. It would have been our forty-fifth wedding anniversary, had we been celebrating it. I skimmed through the document, though it took several moments before I realized what it was. The most unusual thing I'd ever read. A horse breed registry, with the breed typed in:

American Cream Draft Horse

"It's a horse registry," I explained, reading the paperwork aloud.

According to the record, the horse was a mare named Knight Rider and had been purchased by Rick Mallowan in 2019. He'd bought my dream horse—the breed I had told him about back in 1977—and named *her* (of course Rick wouldn't give her a feminine name) after his second favorite on-screen character, Knight Rider (the first being John Wayne, of course).

Why had he never told me? And where the heck was the horse now?

"Wait, there's more." Tara handed me another page.

It was a horse purchase agreement for Knight Rider, three years later, dated April 30, 2022. The buyer names shocked me more than finding out Rick had bought and hidden my dream horse somewhere.

"The seller, Rick Mallowan, agrees to sell the horse known as Knight Rider, an American Cream Draft Horse mare, to Benson Mallowan and Ginger Mallowan, for the sum of $1. Tack and bridle are to be included in sale."

The rest was a bunch of legal jargon and horse registration information, but the main gist of it was that Benson knew about the horse, my name was even on the ownership paperwork, and yet this was the first time I was hearing about it over a year and a half later!

I couldn't really blame Benson for not telling me, since he died only a couple months after this, and things had been a chaotic haze leading up to his death. I suppose it took a lot of time plotting to throw his own mother in a nursing home so he could steal my house out from under me. Not that I was still bitter or anything. My son had paid for his sins with his life, after all.

"Along with a missing husband, you now also have a missing horse to find." Tara headed toward the open door, where Sloane kept looking out at the empty parking lot.

"I think we should go." Sloane, who wasn't afraid of Judge Valance but terrified of creepy-crawlers, appeared worried. "I've seen the same red car pass by twice. I think they're following us."

"You don't have to ask me twice," Tara agreed. "I have no desire to get locked in an abandoned storage unit after dark. Because you know Sloane will be the first to get killed if our night turns into a horror flick."

"Why, because I'm Black?" Sloane's eyebrow lifted.

"No, because you're the hottest. The hot girls always get murdered first," Tara corrected.

Sloane signed a hasty *no no no.* "You're wrong. It's always the dumb blonde first. The first victim is not always the hottest. In which case it would be…" Sloane pretended to mull over whether Tara or I were the dumbest.

"Well certainly not me! As the oldest I'm also the wisest," I insisted.

I had no idea about any of these murder mystery rules, but I also didn't watch horror films. "So there's a rule for who gets killed first in movies based first on hotness, then race?"

"Guys…" Sloane tried to interject with a sign, waving for Tara's attention.

But Tara was already launching into a lengthy explanation about general practices in the horror genre. "Well actually," Tara began, taking a breath, "generally the murder order is first the dumb jock or slutty cheerleader, which could also be the hot and or dumb girl. Next is usually a nerd or person of color, because they have a bad feeling they're going to die and simply have bad luck. If the final girl has a best friend, she'd be next to die."

"The final girl?" I asked.

"You know, the final girl who makes it through until the end," Tara explained. "Anyway, the love interest would be the last victim, since he would be the most emotional loss. Last would be, of course, the final girl. You can spot her a mile away because she's super smart, almost always a virgin, and she either survives or dies right before the end."

"Wow." I huffed. "That's quite an analysis you put together. By that logic, Sloane would be the first hot girl kill, you would be the next best friend kill, and Rick would die close to the end. I'd maybe or maybe not survive in the very last scene," I deduced, then grinned wickedly. "Though, let me tell you, I definitely wouldn't make the virgin cut after the last few months with Rick in my bed!"

Tara grimaced and stuck her fingers in her ears. "La la la

la—"

"Guys!" This time Sloane used her voice, coupled with an insistent wave. "Someone's here!"

Chapter 13

I heard the gunshot before I felt it.

We had finished our search through storage unit 14, only after the fact realizing we had left fingerprints all over what could have been crime scene evidence. Not that I had yet decided what to do about the police. The threat was clear: If I go to the cops, Rick dies. Even though there was blood in the storage unit, it wasn't necessarily Rick's. And even if it was, it didn't mean he was dead. Just relocated. Hopefully not into a grave yet.

After dragging the garage door closed, we snuck halfway across the parking lot toward the rundown sign jutting like a pinnacle from a sea of asphalt. I had just noticed that the sign read *tow Away* instead of *Stow Away* and chuckled to myself, when a red sports car—it could only be the one Sloane had seen—screeched across the pavement outside of the gate. A streetlight illuminated enough to show the driver's-side window roll down, but it was too dark to make out the figure inside the vehicle.

Pop.

It took a moment for me to recognize the sound.

"He's shooting at us!" Tara shrieked.

The rest was a blur of *pop-pop-pop* as Tara and I hit the

ground, while Sloane—not hearing the gunshot—ducked in a delayed reaction. When Sloane finally jumped into action, she looked like a soldier at boot camp, assessing the threat, zigzagging across the lot, and taking cover.

I, on the other hand, had been halfway to the gate when the first bullet was fired, and I was still halfway to the gate out in the wide open when the second, third, and forth zoomed past me. A sittin' duck that was about to be worm food.

I couldn't tell if it was quiet or not with the buzzing in my ears. Pressing myself as far into the ground as concrete would allow, I was afraid to look up to see if the car had left. So I wrapped my arms over my head, as if my frail bones could stop a bullet from exploding through my skull, then I waited.

Another *pop-pop* echoed, as a spray of concrete pelted my chin. The bullet couldn't have hit the ground more than a foot away from me.

I had lost count of the bullets, but I was pretty sure there were more coming, and I was an easy target. Barely lifting my head, I shifted up to my hands and knees and army crawled my way back toward a Dumpster I had spotted earlier. At the least, I was moving, making me a harder target to hit. I hoped.

I had a good ten feet to go before another *pop* pinged the side of the metal Dumpster, where Tara and Sloane had managed to hide behind.

"Hurry, Ginger!" Tara screamed.

By this point I wasn't crawling fast enough to win a race against a sloth, so I jumped to my feet, crouched, and ran as I felt another *pop* pulverize the ground behind me. It was so close, the earth hit my ankles. And then I realized it wasn't close at all.

The bullet had gotten me.

A pain shot up through my leg, searing my nerve endings. Losing the feeling in my foot, I fell to my chest, sprawled out on the ground.

Sloane scooted around Tara, launching herself at me. With a firm grip she grabbed me around the torso, her back to the shooter like a shield, and hefted me upright while I hung limply against her. With a force that contradicted her sinewy shape, Sloane vaulted across the pavement with me into Tara's open arms without even breaking a sweat.

Once Sloane dropped into a crouch beside me, checking my leg for the damage, I started hyperventilating. Was I bleeding out? Would my leg need to get amputated? Would Rick still want me if I didn't have the legs he loved so much? I could feel myself slipping as I tucked my head between my knees and sucked in whatever air would let me.

Sloane cupped my chin and lifted my face to hers. "Ginger, calm down. It's only a graze. Look."

She pointed to a red smear across my ankle, a few inches above my ankle bone. The wound was caught somewhere between a scratch and hole, barely muscle deep. The skin hung loosely around it, and the blood oozing from it made me feel queasy. At least the bullet had made a clean exit.

"Give me your scrunchie," Sloane ordered.

"My scrunchie?" I asked. "I know my hair's a mess, but now is hardly the time for a makeover—"

Sloane didn't let me finish as she tugged my hair free from the huge velvet hair tie and secured it over my wound.

"It will put pressure on it to help stop the bleeding until we get you a proper bandage," Sloane explained.

Who was this bullet-dodging gymnast EMT who couldn't

cook a pot roast but who knew how to dress a gunshot wound? I had never seen this side of Sloane before, but I liked it!

"Do you think they're gone?" I asked. By now the adrenaline had numbed my entire body from tonight's acrobatics. I deftly rose to stand up.

"I don't know," Tara said.

"Did you get the license plate number?" Sloane turned to ask Tara.

"Heck no, I'm not popping my head out. I'm not a Whac-a-Mole game!"

With all three of us tucked out of sight for several minutes now, the shooter must have given up. A moment later I heard a car rev away, while I peered out from my hiding place to see if I could catch the plate number.

It was too dark, and the vehicle fled away too fast. So I flicked him off instead and shouted a curse word that he would never hear because his tires were already spittin' gravel halfway down the road.

"He's gone," I announced.

"Did anyone at least catch the make and model?" Sloane signed.

"Does *new red sports car* count?" I guesstimated.

Tara groaned. "Can we finally involve the police please?" Tara glared at me, and I knew I didn't have a choice in the matter. "We all almost died tonight, and if it's between us or Rick dying, I pick him."

I hoped we would actually get a choice in the matter.

We were finally safe—as safe as one could be with a gunman after us—in the car when I turned to Sloane. I couldn't hold myself back from asking, not after what I had just seen.

"What was all that about, Sloane?"

"All of what?" she asked, so nonchalantly that I almost believed that my eyes were playing tricks on me and nothing had happened.

"Those Lara Croft moves you just did. And standing up to Judge Valance like you were untouchable. Is there something about you I don't know? Like you're secretly a ninja or undercover CIA? Because I really thought you might kill someone. You actually scared me tonight."

Sloane shifted uncomfortably, redirecting her gaze out the window, avoiding an answer. After a strange silence, she spoke, "I guess there's a lot you don't know about me that I hope you never find out."

Something rustled inside me, and I knew she was right. We all had things we hoped no one found out.

Chapter 14

I was surprised to wake up the next morning with only a bruise on my knee, a few scrapes on my palms, and my ankle war wound already scabbing over. Not bad for an old bird besieged in a drive-by shooting!

But the whole thing was too close for comfort, and finding Rick was turning out to be above Tara's Angels' pay grade. I was lucky the bullet only grazed me instead of hitting a major artery, Tara had reminded me a bajillion times. She didn't appreciate my Monty Python "'tis only a flesh wound" retort.

So it had been decided, and I was outnumbered. On our way home from Stow Away, Don't Throw Away Storage, we had *unanimously* decided to go to the police first thing in the morning after we'd had a night of rest, reflection, and recovery. I was guilted into my vote, by the way.

It turned out to be all reflection—with no rest or recovery—as I fretted the hours away until the sky grew pink with dawn.

I eventually caved to the insomnia and headed into my computer room, where I turned to my trusty Pentium computer that had survived Y2K. With a little finetuning from Bennie over the years, it still miraculously ran… slow as dirt, but it still did the job.

I thought back to the man Rick had signed over the title of

his motorcycle to at the rodeo back in '77. He had nearly put Rick in the hospital, making me wonder if there wasn't some unspoken beef between the two.

After an hour of website deep-diving, apparently to find an old motorcycle title I needed a VIN, and to find the VIN I needed the motorcycle or an old property tax bill from that year. It was a catch-22 that sent me down a furious internet search rabbit hole. So the bike that was supposed to be *the key*... turned out to be a dead end.

Grabbing a notebook, I jotted down:

Ask BBPD to look up Rick's DMV motorcycle VIN record for 1977

Maybe the police would have better luck finding the title transfer than I did. That is, if I ended up talking to them this morning. There was still that pesky threat to kill Rick if I went to the authorities. While Tara had been insistent we let Detective Hughes take it from here, it wasn't Tara's husband's life on the line. It was *mine*. So really, did she deserve a say in the matter?

But then again, she did almost get killed because of him. Maybe as long as I stayed away from her and Sloane, they would stay safe... right?

Love—that was my real weakness. I had always believed that love meant standing by—and standing up for—one another no matter what. Love disregarded our blemishes and embraced our quirks, accepting every part of each other.

But that's where the flaw in the logic lived. As much

leniency as love gave us, it let us off the hook too easily. We let those we love hurt us, and in turn we hurt them back and expected forgiveness without accountability. Rick had been doing it to me for years, and I was now doing it to Tara and Sloane.

I had always interpreted love as tolerance, but tolerance could easily turn toxic. I gave myself the freedom to be my worst, most selfish version because of *love*. It was cruel, not kind. And definitely not love.

I decided then and there that I would do the right thing and take Tara with me to hand the reins over to Detective Hughes, the risk to Rick be damned. There was just one loose end I needed to deal with first, then I would let the cards fall where they may.

Chapter 15

There were only two horse boarding facilities in Bloodson Bay where my missing horse could have been hidden. The first—and best, if I do say so myself—was the Rockin' C Ranch horse rescue, which happened to be owned and run by Tara and her sister-in-law Peace.

The other boarding place... well, I shuddered to think of Knight Rider—the name was really growing on me—living there for the past four years since Rick had bought her. There was only one way to find out, but it would require me to play nice with my enemies.

Valance Farms was owned by none other than Judge Ewan Valance, but I didn't dare venture there alone. Not when he could possibly be behind Rick's disappearance, and not when he probably hired the gunman behind our storage unit showdown and the blonde message delivery woman. So I came to the only mediator I knew who was "in" with the Valance family, and who I also trusted, which was a nearly impossible combination.

Peace Christie.

Peace was a storm gale. Fierce, stubborn, and a bit scary if you didn't know her. Growing up on a ranch had made the gal tough as nails, but it was paired with a soft heart for animals and kids. Which made sense, considering her family's history.

Lou and Liz Christie, Peace's parents, had been the golden couple of Bloodson Bay all through the 1980s and 1990s. As mayor, Lou gave everything of himself to our town, oftentimes getting in the proverbial ring with Judge Valance himself in order to protect Bloodson Bay's citizens.

Unlike the Valances, Lou never let this position of power get to his head. As a humble ranching family, they raised their kids to appreciate the land and all that nature had to offer, ever since they inherited it from Lou's parents, and his parents' parents, going back all the way to the original town founders. On top of rescuing horses, they ran the Loving Arms Children's Home, singlehandedly funding the orphanage since the late 1970s, even before they had adopted my son Chris.

The Christies dedicated their lives to saving animals and kids, a sacrificial trait that made them a perfect fit to be my son's adoptive parents. It took me a long while before I came around to see it that way, burning with jealousy that they got to raise my son and have the ideal family that I had always wanted with Rick. Endless poverty, crappy jobs, and a negligent estranged husband eventually set me straight, and I grew to love the Christie family for giving Chris the life I couldn't.

And a little sister he adored.

Chris was protective over Peace, but not enough to get involved in her relationship with Leonard Valance. As long as she was happy, Chris was happy. In my lived-a-lot-of-life wisdom, I tended to disagree, but I was also wise enough to keep my mouth shut when it came to other peoples' relationships. After all, what did I know? I clearly wasn't the leading expert.

The drive winding through the Rockin' C Ranch was

especially beautiful today, the golden fields sun-dappled and wispy. Peace lived at the top of a gently rolling hill, in the same house she had grown up in after inheriting it from her dead parents. A cute house filled with her mother's décor and bittersweet memories that Tara often regaled me with. As Chris's high school sweetheart, Tara forged a friendship with Peace that was as deep as the roots of the shaggy coastal cypress trees that hugged the jagged edge of their property where the land dropped off into the bay.

This morning the pastures were dotted with horses of all kinds, and in all stages of life. Fat foals, skinny rescues, lumbering bow-backed retirees... all of them had a home with lavish love and abundant apples and carrots here.

I stepped up to the front porch, overhearing a scuffle through a screened open window.

"Peace Christie?" I called out as I knocked on her front door and began to turn the doorknob.

Behind the slab of cedar her Great Pyrenees barked, and I instinctively released the knob and stepped back. At shy of a hundred pounds large, Puffin was one ball of white fluff I had no desire to catch by surprise.

"Peace, it's Ginger Mallowan!" I rapped on the door again, hearing a shallow voice echoing from inside.

I couldn't make out the words over the dog barking. I waited a minute for Puffin to calm down.

"Help me!" I heard this time. It was Peace, followed by a racket deep within the house.

Puffin barked even more enthusiastically.

"Uh, I can't get in!" I yelled at the wood.

Another crash was followed by a scream. I was fixin' to get

mauled, but whatever was going on inside sounded urgent.

I turned the handle and opened the door a crack, stooping down to meet Puffin eye to eye, in case she happened to remember me.

"Hey, Puffin!" I greeted her chipperly.

A growl and show of teeth convinced me she didn't consider me a friend.

I remembered the biscuits I had wrapped up and put in my purse from Luna's two days ago. I didn't think Puffin would mind if it was a little… crunchy. I slid the stale offering through the slit, and she gobbled it down like it was her last meal on death row.

"We cool now?" I asked her.

She barked once in my face, spraying me with dog spit that smelled like she'd eaten cow patties for breakfast, then managed to slip her tongue through the crack and landed a lick on my cheek. It felt safe to say if Puffin hadn't remembered me as the *Treat Lady* before, she would from now on. Or as long as a dog's short-term memory lasted.

I let myself in, noticing a baby gate blocking Puffin inside the living room, which explained why she failed to come to Peace's rescue, wherever Peace was in the house.

"Peace?" It was a sound just above a whisper.

"In… here…" she grunted, so I followed the direction of her voice.

Stealthily making my way through the living room, over the baby gate, and into the kitchen, I saw Peace hunched over on the floor with a scattering of Tupperware and kitchen gadgets around her.

She didn't move for a long second, then suddenly she began

thrashing.

"Peace!" I scurried over and around the fallen kitchenware toward her.

"I need your help," she grunted.

"What in the Sam Hill is going on?" I rushed to her side just as she flailed back, nearly knocking me over.

Then she suddenly popped upright, out of breath. "I could use an extra set of hands."

When I finally realized what exactly she was doing, I couldn't believe my eyes. Or my ears.

A loud *quack* resonated through the kitchen as it dawned on me that she was wrestling a... duck?

"Come again?" If Peace wanted help butchering a duck, she was asking the wrong country gal. Blood and I didn't get along; I fainted the last time I saw a nose bleed.

"I'm trying to diaper this guy, but he's being stubborn," Peace explained, but she may as well have been explaining the Theory of Relativity.

"Diaper what?"

"He's my house duck. He's not allowed outside due to an injury, so he needs to be diapered so he doesn't poop all over my floors. He's usually good about getting his diaper on, but today he's being fussy."

Quack, quack!

I knew how sharp those webbed ducky claws actually were. Did I mention *I didn't like blood*? But if I wanted Peace's help, I'd better suck it up and hold the darn duck.

He was slicker than snot on a doorknob. It took a good five minutes before we were able to secure the cutest duck diaper I'd ever seen, designed and handmade by Peace and sold on Etsy.

After that debacle, I didn't feel so bad asking for a favor in return.

"So what do you need?" Peace knew me well enough to know I didn't diaper a duck without an ulterior motive.

"It involves the Valances…" I hesitated as her eyebrow cocked.

She had made it perfectly clear that when it came to the Valance family, she wanted no part of any drama. Her and her boyfriend had vocally opted out of the family tension.

It all began when Peace started dating Leonard Valance, the son of Judge Ewan Valance, which none of us were fond of, especially Tara. The feud between the Christie and Valance families spanned two hundred years, rooted in land disputes, petty jealousies, and of course throw in some unrequited love.

Tara wanted me to side with her, but then again, I married Rick, who had worked for the Valances and I'm sure had buried bodies for them, so I wasn't in a position to take sides.

While my disdain for the corrupt Judge was no secret, I tried my best to play it neutral when it came to Peace and Leonard's love life. I rode the fence, for both Tara and Peace's sakes. But there was one thing I knew that Peace didn't, and I had been forbidden from telling her… for now:

Her buff beau Leonard was a liar.

The worst kind of liar.

Not the little white lie kind of liar who fibbed about going to the grocery store for milk but instead went to the bar for beer. No, Leonard was the double-crossing kind of liar, one who would throw his own brother under the bus to save himself.

Three decades ago, at the orders of his father, teenage Leonard had abducted Sloane's mother, Alika, and let his brother Victor take the fall. By the time news of the abduction came out six months ago, Victor was already dead and couldn't defend his name. But Tara, Sloane, and I found out the truth—that Leonard was the one who had done it—and a set of cassette tapes with Leonard's teenage voice on them were the only proof of his crime.

Only after assuring Alika we would protect her did she finally step forward, publicly pointing a finger at Judge Valance for what he had done to her.

Initially we wanted her to turn Leonard in. But there was that pesky problem of Tara not wanting to break her sister-in-law's heart, who it seemed had finally found love... in the wrong place, with the wrong family. Leonard Valance, of all people. Since he had been a young teenager doing his father's bidding, we went back and forth on whether to turn him in, hoping he would do the right thing and come forward on his own about his crimes. Instead, his lips remained sealed as his silence helped defend his guilty father.

An aiding and abetting liar, that's what Peace's boyfriend was. And now I was supposed to play pretend that all was fine and dandy as I approached him about my missing horse.

"What do you need from the Valances?" Peace exhaled a long breath as if expecting the worst.

I bit back what I really wanted to say, that the man she was dating had committed an atrocity, that he was just like his dreadful father, but I didn't. Instead I said, "I need you to come with me to Valance Farms as a buffer. I think there's a horse there that belongs to me. An American cream draft."

Peace whistled. She knew how rare a breed it was. And how reluctant the Valances would be to part with it.

"Sure, I'll go with you. But I should warn you, if Ewan is there, you won't be any safer with me. He's gunning for you, Ginger."

Boy did I know it. But I had something he didn't.

Chapter 16

Ewan Valance had everything to lose, while I had nothing left. That little detail gave me all the control.

Until I walked into the Valance Farms barn and all that control vanished.

Never underestimate the power of a man with his shirt off. Or the hormones of a lonely woman.

Leonard Valance's pants were so tight I could see his religion. For the briefest of moments I could understand what Peace saw in him. Especially with the kind of abs you only got as man familiar with good old-fashioned manual labor.

Lord help me, he could fry eggs on that stomach! But just because someone looked good on the outside didn't mean they were good on the inside. In fact, I usually found it to be quite the opposite with most people.

Leonard was in the middle of mucking stalls when we had pulled up to the barn. Near the house I spotted Judge Ewan Valance. Hopped up on excitement and audacity, I gave him a cheeky wave hello and blew him a kiss.

He flicked me off in return.

Peace grabbed my arm and shook her head. "Stop it! You're asking for trouble."

Trouble might as well have been my middle name.

Inside one of the stalls we found Leonard, the perfect movie-star Western cowboy, his chest smeared with sweat and dirt in all its chiseled glory. Beneath his cowboy hat his smile lit up as Peace entered the barn, then it drooped as I appeared behind her.

"Ms. Mallowan," he greeted me coldly.

At least he had the manners to address an elder properly to my face. But that didn't mean he wouldn't kill me the moment I turned my back.

"Leonard," I replied in kind. "I thought you had... *minions* to do your dirty work."

Peace shot me a glare, but I couldn't stop myself from getting a dig in.

"What makes you think I don't mind getting my hands dirty?" I didn't like the dark tone in Leonard's voice.

Ain't that the truth, I thought but knew better than to say out loud.

"Play nice, kids." Peace sounded as awkward as she looked. "Leo, Ginger's here about a horse. An American cream draft mare."

"You got proof of ownership?" Leonard set aside his shovel, hooking his finger in his jeans belt loop.

"I have the papers right here." I rummaged through my purse, found them, and handed them over.

Leonard read it slowly, probably trying to look for any loophole to keep my horse, then handed it back to me.

"Does my dad know Ginger's here?" he asked Peace.

"Don't know, don't care," I interjected. "I just want to get my horse and go."

"You know, it could be considered abandonment that you

109

never came forward to claim your horse before now. Plus no one's been paying for her boarding fees for over a year. So technically, I think I have a case for claiming ownership, considering what you owe." Leonard threw the threat out there, but I wasn't biting. I knew the value of this horse.

Bennie must have been writing the checks, which obviously stopped when he died. Legally Leonard had a point, but I couldn't let him win. Not this time.

"I guess I'll camp out then, because I'm not leaving without my horse."

"Then pay the boarding fee balance and we'll talk," Leonard argued.

The bill had to be in the thousands by now. I had to find a way to appeal to this greedy douchebag who was so quick to take advantage of an old lady.

"What if I let you breed her? We'll split the profit," I suggested.

"Leo, come on. Don't be like your dad," Peace pleaded.

I watched Leonard soften, glad Peace had agreed to come with me, along with lending me her horse trailer, since I sure as heck wasn't going to fit a horse in my mid-size car.

"Deal." Leonard extended his hand and I shook it, ever so tentatively. It felt like making a deal with the devil. "So Knight Rider belongs to you, then? You're one lucky lady."

I didn't know if *lucky* was the right word to describe me, considering in the past three days my husband went missing, I'd been shot at, and I kept getting mysterious threats in the mail. But hey, I had my dream horse!

Why would Rick and Bennie have kept her away from me for so long? What was the big deal with keeping everything around her so hush-hush? It didn't make sense.

"Has she been here for four years?" I asked, hoping Leonard might be able to fill in some of the blanks.

"Yep. Rick brought her here back when he first got her. He said she was a gift for his lady. I'm guessing he was referring to you."

"Go any idea why I'm only hearing about her now?"

"Oh, I sure do," Leonard said with a weak laugh. "Your husband was on the run."

My heart battered against my chest.

"From who?"

"Bratva, last I heard."

I choked on the shock. "The Russian mob?" How deep had Rick dug himself into this mess?

"Apparently he stole something he shouldn't have and had to go into hiding. Then one day Rick shows up out of the blue and tells me his son Benson is gonna take over the boarding payments. Never got a dime from him, by the way."

That was no surprise. Benson liked animals as much as Sloane liked spiders. He sure as heck wouldn't pay to keep one alive.

"Anyway, I'm guessing Benson was supposed to let you know about the horse and never did."

"As you know, he died right around that time," I said wistfully.

A glimpse of sympathy crossed Leonard's face. "Sorry for your loss. I forgot about that. I guess that's why he only showed up at the barn one time, then I never saw him here again."

I could kill Bennie for not telling me about her... if he wasn't already dead!

"Anyway, you ready to meet your new horse?"

Leonard led the way through several rows of stalls, beautifully painted with ornate detailing that put the Rockin' C Ranch's bare-bones barn to shame. When we arrived at Knight Rider's stall, she was as beautiful as I imagined. Huge, at least two tons, and a milky golden color. She nuzzled me as if she knew I was her long-lost mama, pressing her velvety nose against my cheek as I ran my hand down her neck.

I was in love. A way more reliable love than I'd ever had with Rick. She was a dream come true!

"The paperwork says she came with some tack. A bridle and saddle. Where are those at?" I asked.

"I'll grab everything for you and meet you at Peace's trailer. I'm assuming you're taking her to..." He stopped, as if the *Rockin' C Ranch* was a dirty word.

"Yes, Leo, bring her to my farm. We'll discuss the breeding terms once she's all settled in," Peace said.

Leonard glanced outside the huge barn door toward the house.

"We best do this around back in case my dad's hanging around. This is the last thing I want him to see. And for the love of God, Ginger, stay out of his line of sight or you'll be in a world of trouble."

Oops. I was pretty sure I already was.

Part 2
Tara Christie

WHAT SHE DOESN'T KNOW

Chapter 17

Owning a farm was a love-hate relationship. The sprawling fields that dropped off the cliff overlooking the bay. The wildflowers speckling the land with color. The lush wood line fragrant with wet, earthy leaves. The sunset that painted the sky pink. The scent of fresh-cut hay. Watching the horses gallop across the field as they neighed and played. This was my life and I loved all of it.

Most of the time.

On the *hate* side of the relationship were the endless outdoor chores, rain or shine, that grew blisters on my hands. The dirty stalls I had to clean daily. The injury Havoc had gotten from trying to break through the fence that I had to clean and wrap. The broken fence that I now had to fix. The constant mowing and planting and demands that made taking a vacation impossible. And right now, I felt desperate for a vacation.

A *babymoon*, to be precise.

My pregnancy was at the point where I felt exhausted most of the time, and when I wasn't exhausted, I was losing focus of what I was running around doing that was making me even more exhausted. My feet were swollen, my back ached, and my brain frazzled. All I wanted was a little getaway with Chris to recharge my energy and replenish our love.

But with Ginger's new horse to accommodate, and The Case of Ginger's Missing Husband to solve, that babymoon looked more distant than ever.

At least Chris would be coming home today from his out-of-town job interview... and if everything worked out as planned, he could work remotely from home and life could stay as intact as possible. But that was a pretty big *if.*

If the job didn't work out, we'd have to move. Start over somewhere new. Step down from running the Loving Arms Children's Home. Maybe even shut down Rockin' C Ranch.

It wasn't exactly the worst possible scenario, but leaving Ginger and Sloane, while my daughter Nora would be starting college next year and a new baby on the way... it was a lot of change for a gal who had never stepped foot out of Small Town, USA.

"Tara, take a picture of me with Knight Rider."

Ginger handed me her phone, posing with one arm slung over the horse's huge head and puckering up in the long-outdated kissy lips pose that Ginger thought the cool kids were still doing.

I didn't tell her that pose went out of style along with wedge sneakers and harem pants.

Remnants of the sunset glistened off the gem accents on the bridle, competing with the sparkle of joy in Ginger's green eyes. This horse might be exactly what Ginger needed to heal from all the damage life had done to her.

The dome of the sun's head faded into the sea as we finished unloading Knight Rider into her new stall. Soaking in the breeze that lingered with the scent of ocean, I dropped down onto a hay bale to catch my breath and rest my swollen body. I had forgotten how demanding a rutabaga-sized fetus could be.

"I can't believe I faced off with the devil and won!" Ginger smirked. "I gave Ewan Valance a little *eff you*, Ginger-style."

"I don't want to know." Though I kinda did. I just didn't want to encourage her. "You just love to poke the bear, don't you?"

"Only the mean ones."

I had to admit, I was both fearful yet proud that Ginger had managed to escape the Valance Farm unscathed.

"Don't be too quick to celebrate. That man has a long memory, and even longer patience," I warned.

Patient people dished out the worst revenge.

I slowly rose to my feet and grabbed her horse's saddle and bridle, carrying them to the tack room. The horse was impressive and in ideal condition. Even the saddle was a well-cared-for rich cognac leather with gorgeous detailing. But the bridle—that alone was unlike anything I'd seen.

"I recognize this craftmanship. This is Rick's leather work," Ginger said, examining it with awe. "He had to have made this bridle specifically for me."

Bedecked across the leather browband were shiny green jewels that matched Ginger's eyes. It didn't look cheap or manufactured. The contrast stitching definitely looked custom made. I had boarded horses for years for some high-end owners, and I'd seen pretty fancy riding gear, but this was something else. Rick had taken bedazzling to a whole new level, and it matched Ginger's sparkly personality perfectly.

"What's the deal with this horse, anyway? I don't understand why you're just now finding out about her. Why do you think Rick never told you?"

The whole thing felt shady. As Ginger inadequately explained, Rick had bought Ginger's dream horse with the intention of giving it to her for their anniversary. When he was forced to go on the run, he took off, leaving the horse behind and forgotten for three years.

Somehow he had reconnected with Benson, signing the horse over to him and Ginger. But Benson died within two months, and once again the horse was forgotten. But Rick had been back in Ginger's life for six months now. How had the topic of the horse not come up?

It was all so cloak-and-dagger... but *why*?

"I'm still trying to figure that out." Ginger examined the bridle, resting her fingertip in a divot on the top strap. The divot wasn't shaped like the others, rather it was an odd, irregular shape. "Hm, I just noticed one of the rhinestones is missing. I wonder if it fell off in the Valance's barn."

"If you're hinting for me to go look for it, no can do. It's getting late and I'm supposed to meet Sloane this evening, and I've got to pick Chris up from the airport in..." I checked the time on my phone. "Yikes! In less than an hour. I've gotta get you home and head to the airport. Ask Peace to take you."

"I think Peace has had enough of me for one day."

As we walked to my truck, Ginger's phone pinged with a text. A look of worry creased her brow.

"Everything okay?" I asked.

She frowned. "I don't know. Sloane says she needs to talk, and it's urgent."

Sloane never used the word *urgent* unless it was, well, urgent. "Do you want me to drop you off there instead of at home?"

I stepped up into the driver's seat with a grunt. I felt utterly drained. And the evening was just beginning. I was supposed to head over to Sloane's to plan a fall festival party for the Loving Arms Children's Home, but I was running out of time. And energy.

Another ping came from deep in Ginger's never-ending purse. It was a true miracle how much she could fit in there, like a clown purse but instead of squirting flowers and endless ribbons of silk, it was sewing kits and tissues... and I think I even saw a biscuit in there?

"Yeah, take me to Sloane's. It sounds like something bad happened," Ginger agreed.

"I'll be passing her house anyway. Can you tell her I need to cancel our party planning meeting tonight? I'm running late to pick Chris up from the airport, and I'm not sure I'll have the energy to add anything more to my to-do list tonight."

"Ooh, got plans for a romantic date tonight?" Ginger teased.

"There is nothing romantic about swollen feet and underboob sweat," I lamented. "Did Sloane give any idea of what's going on?"

With her mother testifying against Ewan Valance about her abduction, I had worried he might try to retaliate. Or silence her... for good. In Bloodson Bay, you never knew what lurked in the shadows or hid behind the corner.

Ginger's phone pinged one last time.

"All she said was, 'You need to come right away.' Whatever it is, it just went from urgent to dire."

I wanted to be there for Sloane, if today didn't kill me first.

Chapter 18

The airport *terminal* was aptly named.

After waiting for thirty minutes, I was instructed by security to keep circling the airport until Chris arrived at the exit so I wouldn't block other cars picking up their loved ones.

I had barely seen another set of headlights at our tiny airfield that was generously called an airport, let alone enough cars to warrant putting me on an endless driving loop. But after forty-five minutes of wasting gas, and getting no reply from Chris to my texts or voicemails, I decided to park and head inside.

Clear plastic sheets draped from the ceiling down the middle of the building where apparently construction was under way… without a construction worker in sight. Ladders and buckets were precariously placed over drop cloths that the handful of airport employees walked across. This place looked anything but professional.

The sole assistant at the only service desk in the single room that comprised the Bloodson Bay Airport looked ready for bed as she rolled her eyes when I approached. She was no help at all in figuring out where Chris's flight was, or why it was running over an hour late, according to the screen listing the remaining flights for the day.

"Our system is running slow," she barely explained. "Sorry

I can't be of more help." She certainly didn't sound sorry, though.

At this point the Caesar salad I had eaten for lunch was long gone, despite the lingering taste of garlic that made me want to vomit—or were those my pregnancy hormones amping up again? Regardless, things were about to get *terminal* if I didn't get answers.

"So you have no idea where my husband's flight is? How does an airplane just go missing and unaccounted for?" I had lost all pleasantness in my tone. I just wanted my husband and a nap.

"I'm sorry, ma'am, but all it's showing is that his flight is delayed. There's nothing else I can do. Now if you'll step aside, I need to help other customers." The assistant had lost all pleasantness in her tone as well, not that she had much friendliness to begin with.

I glanced behind me, where one fancy-suit man stood in line. *One.* He shoved me aside so he could book a ticket to somewhere beautiful and relaxing and extravagant.

My phone rang, and my heart inflated as I rummaged through my purse to take Chris's call. However, it didn't turn out to be Chris, but Ginger. I didn't have time for her right now; I had my own crisis to manage. Like the nausea rolling around in my stomach. I declined the call and checked the flight schedule on the wall, which still said *Delayed.*

A moment later my phone chimed with a text, then another and another. What the heck was the emergency this time?

I'm still at Sloane's.
Come ASAP.

Something's wrong.

I tucked my phone into my back pocket, which was inching precariously close to splitting the seams at this point in my pregnancy. Was it getting hot in here? Definitely enough that I wanted to take off all my clothes, as Nelly so accurately sang. I unbuttoned the top button of my jeans, rolled up my sleeves, and hip-checked the fancy suit out of line. I was done being semi-polite.

"Look, lady, I'm pregnant and cranky—"

"I can see that," she muttered under her breath.

"—and I just want to know if I should go home or wait for my husband. My feet are killing me, my husband is jobless, our horse rescue is going under, my daughter will be starting college next year, and I have a *baby* on the way, which I'm totally not ready for, especially with no income, and it would mean the world to me if you'd just give me five minutes of your time to find out what's going on with my husband's flight."

By the time I finished my tirade I was sobbing, and scaring fancy suit away, blaming it on the hormones or exhaustion or stress or all of the above. But whatever the cause, it seemed to work as the lady held up a finger and picked up the phone.

"I'll get you some answers, ma'am."

Ten minutes later I found out the worst possible scenario that any wife could imagine.

Chapter 19

I never considered a bomb threat on a plane being something I'd ever experience personally, or applying to my own family. While September 11, 2001, had brought that very real threat to surface for many Americans, it had always felt so removed from me as I sat tucked away in my quiet little town when the Two Towers fell, or when Flight 93 crashed.

Now it felt as real as the day was long.

The desk assistant sounded as terrified as I felt. She looked too young to have lived through 9/11. Her hands trembled as she hung up the phone. This was probably the closest she'd ever gotten to a genuine emergency.

"This is strictly confidential," her voice shook as she spoke, "but all they were willing to tell me was that there was a bomb threat on your husband's flight. I don't have any more information than that."

"Oh my gosh. A bomb? I don't... I don't understand." Everything felt jumbled in my head.

"I'm so sorry, ma'am. I don't know what to say."

Neither did I.

"Was it just a threat?" I persisted. "Or was the bomb... detonated? They'd tell you if the plane actually blew up, right?"

"I'm assuming that if there was indeed an actual bomb, and

it had gone off, it would be all over the news by now," she guessed.

That was a pretty huge assumption.

"It was probably just a threat, and it's still under investigation," she continued, offering me nothing but fear on a platter. "If you give me your phone number, I'll personally call you the moment I hear something. But the airline will also be contacting you, along with the authorities who are investigating. You'll get answers soon, I promise."

The worst part was I was terrified to get answers. Answers meant knowing, and knowing meant whatever happened couldn't be undone. What if Chris's plane had exploded—with my husband on it?

I gave her my contact information and wandered back to my truck in a haze, shaking and faint and terrified. Finally in the quiet of my truck cab, my brain slowed enough for me to send Chris a text, just in case he was alive and fine and stranded at another airport.

I love you and am praying that everything's okay. Please call or text the minute you get this. I'm worried sick.

It could be hours before I heard anything, and it was already late, so I decided to head to Sloane's, where Ginger was waiting for me to pick her up. I didn't want to be alone with my head full of worst-case scenarios.

By the time I pulled up Sloane's long driveway it was pitch-black outside, and her isolated glass house was equally dark inside. I found Ginger sitting on the porch, alone, as my headlight beams skirted over her wilted form.

I got out of my truck, greeted by the crashing waves along the rear of Sloane's property. As my feet crunched along the gravel path that led to her porch, Ginger lifted her head weakly.

"What are you doing outside?" I asked.

"Sloane either isn't home or she's already asleep. And her mom isn't answering the door either."

Alika had moved in with Sloane temporarily until the Valance trial was over. Partly because Sloane wanted to keep her mom safe, and partly because Alika wanted to keep her daughter safe. No matter how independent our children got, or how far away they lived, they were always our babies and that mama bear instinct to protect them never left. I still experienced this with Nora, even though she would be heading off to college soon.

"You've been waiting here alone all this time?" I asked. "Do you know what happened that was so urgent?"

"This." Ginger held out a box, and I could take an educated guess of what was inside: another newspaper clipping.

"Sloane had gotten one of my newspaper ads on her porch today. She texted me about it, but when I got here the door was locked, the lights were off, and the ad was just sitting on the porch."

I walked along the side of the house toward the garage. On my tiptoes, I peeked in, seeing her car parked where it always was. Heading further around the house to the back porch, everything was deathly silent except for the ocean, angrily beating the strand tonight. After walking up the porch steps, I pressed my hands to the glass and peered inside, but it was dark and empty.

"I'm sure she's just in bed," I said. "Maybe you're overthinking it. Did you check Instagram to see if maybe Sloane went out of town today for one of her party planning things? She might have taken an Uber to the airport."

The airport. I didn't want to think about that right now.

I knew it was an illogical solution the moment it came out of my mouth, because she hadn't mentioned it last night, and I was supposed to meet with Sloane today. Plus she had texted Ginger to come over. But if not an impromptu trip, then what?

"I don't have social media," Ginger replied.

I checked Sloane's social media account, scrolling through pictures and video feeds. At the top, dated four days ago, I saw one of Sloane and Alika at a beach resort.

"Look." I held up the phone, handing it to Ginger. "Sloane took her mom to the beach. It says here her mom is enjoying a long overdue vacation. So at least we know why her mom isn't here. As for Sloane, she's probably in bed."

Ginger looked at the picture, then handed the phone back.

"That was four days ago, Tara. Sloane texted me hours ago, asking me to meet her. And now she's not here. Why would she ask me to come over, then go to sleep?"

Ginger was right. My gut was right. It wasn't like Sloane at all. But her house looked completely secure and locked. No broken windows or doors. Nothing that *looked* suspicious… from first glance.

"I think something happened to her." Ginger stated what we both were trying to avoid thinking. "We need to go to the police."

"Don't they usually have a policy that the person has to be

missing for at least twenty-four hours?" I reminded her.

"Then we'll show them what the clipping says. Once they see this, there's no way they'll be able to ignore us."

I had completely forgotten about the clipping.

"I'm afraid to ask, but what does it say?"

Chapter 20

BLOODSON BAY BULLETIN
December 3, 1979

WOMEN BOOKKEEPERS NEEDED!

Exciting new careers in bookkeeping are giving thousands of lonely women like you a new outlook on life. And you don't have to be smart to get started!

Everything is explained by experts in easy-to-understand language. We train you at home in <u>your</u> spare time, and your <u>husband</u> won't even miss dinner. You get an automatic electric adding machine and an instant-action pocket-size electronic calculator so you don't have to worry about being good at arithmetic.

<u>Was</u> your shot at a career ruined by your <u>k</u>ids? Don't feel <u>ill</u> about ba<u>d</u> luck! <u>You</u> <u>are</u> the perfect candidate. Take the <u>next</u> step to becoming a bookkeeper today!

We had made our way down to the beach where we could talk in private, in case our nefarious newsie was lurking around the woods surrounding Sloane's house.

A mist rolled along the shore, shivery and viscous, haloing the glow from my phone as I pointed it to guide our path. Ghost crabs scampered around our toes, burrowing into the sand as the flashlight passed over them. Lightning bugs blinked over the dune grass and among the live oaks, their tiny circles of light muted by the fog. So much life, even in the empty darkness.

A new moon had arrived, hiding the lunar disk completely from view, creating an unnatural pit of darkness as the rock sat directly between Earth and the sun.

I gazed up at the sky, taking a moment to admire the spattering of stars above. Further down the beach a cluster of clouds sparked with heat lightning. A distant boom echoed, far enough that I wasn't in a hurry to leave, but close enough to keep an eye on the clouds' path.

A prick of light streaked across the sky as a shooting star crossed directly above me. I hoped that my wish—for Chris to come home safely—would be granted.

"What's it say, Ginger?"

I rested my chin on her shoulder, reading over her with my phone flashlight.

She sniffed.

"Caesar salad for lunch, Tara?" Ginger guessed correctly, shrugging my head off of her bony collarbone.

"How'd you know?" I cupped my hand over my mouth, exhaled, and smelled my breath. Okay, it was *that* obvious.

"Darlin'. Your breath could peel the shell off a crawdad." She ran her chewed fingernail along the illuminated patch of underlined letters and words. "It's another cryptic message."

"What's the message say?" I probed.

"Hold your horses," Ginger replied. "I'm still working on it."

The letters bounced and bobbed as Ginger trembled, holding the page out and squinting to read them. Eventually the words came together:

your husband was k ill d you are next

"*Your husband was ill. You are next,*" Ginger whispered, repeating the marked words verbatim. "Lord have mercy, Rick's sick! And it's contagious! Do you think whatever he has is deadly?"

"Huh?" I pulled the clipping from her grasp and read it for myself. "Oh, honey, that can't be what that says."

I wrapped my arm around her as her shudders pulsed against me.

"I told you to get your eyes checked. Why won't you get some eyeglasses?"

"I don't need them. I can spot a tick on a coon hound from a country mile."

Ginger insisted on still having 20/20 vision that her squinting implied otherwise, worried it would cost her the job as Head Watcher of the neighborhood lookout. Not that anyone had any intention of asking her to relinquish her self-appointed duties, since no one else had the time, or desire, to wander aimlessly around the neighborhood like a Peeping Tom.

"Well, then you'd clearly see that it says…" I paused, silently rereading the message. "Oh. I'm so sorry, Ging."

"Why? What's the bad news?"

I refused to meet her gaze as I mumbled, "Your husband was *killed*."

"What the—? No, that can't be." Ginger grew unnaturally silent, as if the reality had just now occurred to her that Rick might be dead.

But then another thought hit me. Maybe it wasn't about Rick. It wasn't found at Ginger's house, after all. But Sloane's. Where I was *supposed* to have gone today to plan a party for the children's home. I had even mentioned it yesterday outside of Debbie's Diner.

Where Judge Valance had been. And the mysterious blonde woman we had yet to identify. Which proved we were being watched and eavesdropped in on.

Another bolt of lightning split the sky. A crack of thunder pealed across the night air. I glanced up, seeing a larger mound of clouds gathering. The storm was closing in, a big one, and with it being hurricane season, east coasters didn't take these things lightly.

"Do you think this is talking about Rick…" I hesitated as I caught myself speaking the unspeakable. "Or do you think this is referring to Chris?" A panic lifted my voice.

The flight that Chris—my husband, Ginger's son—was supposed to arrive on had been threatened with a bomb. It looked like Ginger's stalker was expanding his efforts to target people close to her. Who else would he go after next—my daughter Nora?

"No, honey, don't think like that." Ginger was trying to

mask the fear, but I heard it in the tremble of her voice. "There's no way this is talking about Chris."

I stumbled back, tears filling my eyes. "But that's what criminals do! They target the loved ones. They could have gotten to Chris in order to make Rick do something for them!"

"Whoever it is," Ginger said, "it's probably just an intimidation tactic. I mean, these are criminals we're dealing with. They're professional liars. I'm sure Chris is fine. And Rick too."

We still hadn't figured out what they wanted, though. And we had followed all of their instructions so far and not gone to the police... unless Ginger wasn't telling me something.

"Did you go to the police, Ginger? I need to know the truth."

"I swear on Bennie's grave, Tara, I haven't told anyone anything. The only people who know are you, me, and... Sloane."

Both our mouths dropped simultaneously.

"Do you think Sloane told the cops, and that's why she's missing?" Ginger speculated.

"We don't know she's missing yet. All we know is she's not answering her door."

But I knew Sloane's doorbell setup. When her doorbell button was pressed, lights flashed all through the house. She even had a vibrational mattress that would shake her bed. Certainly she wouldn't be able to sleep through that.

I looked at the article again, demanding the message give me answers. December 3, 1979, meant something to me, but I couldn't remember what exactly.

"What about the December date? Does it have any significance?" I asked.

"I don't recall anything momentous about it," Ginger replied.

I flipped over the ad, and on the back were two partial news articles. The first one mentioned a local armed robbery that ended up putting the victim in a coma. The other news article covered The Who concert disaster, where eleven fans were killed during a crowd rush. I pointed these out to Ginger.

"Do you remember either of these happening?"

"Oh my gosh," she whispered. "I sure do remember The Who concert. I was there—at the Riverfront Coliseum in Cincinnati, Ohio. Back then Rick and I went to every concert we could afford. Wannabe groupies. I just remember the ambulances before the show, but they didn't even cancel it. The show must go on, as they say. Though Rick and I hit the road halfway through so we could get home before morning. That, and I wanted to avoid the chaos. I wasn't so much of a fan that I was willing to get crushed to death over a rock band."

"Do you think the message has something to do with that?"

Ginger looked skeptical. "I don't see how. What's the connection? Is our stalker a Who fan?" She dropped to the sand, hiding her face in her hands. "I don't know what to do, Tara."

"You know what we have to do, Ginger."

It was the only thing left to do.

"But we can't tell the police or else—"

"Or else what?" I yelled.

A gust of storm wind yelled back, while the ocean waves grew louder and more intense.

"We have no other choice," I screamed over nature, who was doing everything in her power to drown me out. "Someone is *dead*, Chris's plane was threatened with a bomb, Rick is still

MIA, we can't reach Sloane, and we're not getting any closer to figuring this out. We need to go to the police. Now! Before things get any worse."

There were too many people in my life that I cared about to take any more chances. I couldn't stop from envisioning this threat spreading to Nora, my brother, my mom, Sloane's mom...

"Alika," I sputtered. "We need to tell Alika that we can't reach Sloane. If Judge Valance is behind this, and he's got Sloane, there's only one thing he wants... and I'll bet he'll do anything to get it."

My stare met Ginger's. I could see realization turning in that red head of hers.

"If he wants to stop Alika from testifying, this would be the way to do it."

Chapter 21

The rain came swift and heavy, flooding the main roads home from Sloane's and forcing me to take detours that wound through slick back-country mud roads. Ginger's calls to Alika wouldn't connect due to network outages. We had no way to warn her.

After dropping Ginger off at home next door, I parked my truck in the driveway, hoping for a break in the rain that would never come. I waited in the cab of my truck, hypnotized by the watery cascade, noticing something wasn't quite right about the house.

Sheets of rain blew in through the wide-open front door. The house was dark, but I knew I had left the kitchen light on. Then a beam of light panned across the living room window.

It flickered.

Then went black.

It could have been Nora home for a surprise visit from Myrtle Beach, where she was homeschooling under my mom's tutelage for her senior year of high school. It had worked out that Nora was able to take community college courses that would be credited toward her future college degree. But my mom would have checked the weather and postponed a trip, rather than drive through a storm, I would think.

Only a burglar—or a Valance, though they were often one and the same—would leave the door open in the rain, and the lights off while rummaging around in the dark.

I checked my cell phone, debating who to call. The lack of service bars shut that option down, so I shoved down my pregnancy brain fears and hoped for the best.

Making a dash for it, I jumped out of my truck and ran for the house, pausing under the porch roof before going inside where I wasn't sure what I would find. The street was dark, all homes shuttered closed for the night, the windows black, my neighbors off to sweet slumber. Nothing seemed out of the ordinary for this late hour… until I stared through the downpour a few houses down.

I only caught glimpses of it during flashes of lightning that lit up the street. A parked car.

Flash. Red.

Flash. Sporty. Just like the one we'd seen at Stow Away, Don't Throw Away Storage.

My heart raced. I opened up my cell phone to call 9-1-1, but now it was dead. Dead, dead, dead. The word kept echoing in my mind.

I crept into the house, figuring out how I could slip undetected to the gun safe hidden in my bedroom. I slunk through the entry, searching the living room then the kitchen for the beam of light, but the intruder had apparently moved on. I jiggled the back door knob. Locked.

So the intruder was still somewhere in the house.

I grabbed a butcher knife and tiptoed upstairs in the dark, worried about startling whoever was lurking in the shadows.

The blonde messenger?

The shooter?

The newspaper delivery stalker?

When I stepped up on the second-story landing, I noticed the flashlight beam in my bedroom—where my weapon of choice was locked in the gun safe. A knife would have to do, though I prayed I wasn't bringing a knife to a gunfight.

Slipping around the corner of the bedroom door, I peeked in and saw a light in the bathroom. Which seemed an odd place for an intruder to search. What the heck was he looking in there for? My deodorant?

As I approached the bedside table where the gun safe was hidden, I heard a creak directly behind me. Turning around, I came face-to-face with a blinding phone flashlight and I screamed bloody murder while my lurker jumped back.

"Geez, Tara! What is wrong with you?" Chris yelled.

The knife clattered to the floor and I bent over, clutching my chest and sucking in air.

"Are you trying to kill me?" I said between breaths. "You're lucky I didn't stab you again!"

The last time Chris had snuck up on me in the dark I had almost given him a fatal wound to the abdomen. You'd think he would have learned his lesson by now not to go creeping around like a prowler.

"Why didn't you turn on the lights like a normal person?" I asked, reaching for a hug I desperately needed and he willingly gave.

"The storm must have knocked out the electricity." Chris removed his glasses, covered with rain droplets, and wiped them dry with his shirt.

"I'm so glad you're home." Pressing my lips to his cheek, I

felt the implication of scruff where he hadn't shaved. The fear of losing my husband felt like a fresh wound.

"You know I'll always come home, don't you?" Chris must have seen how shaken up I was as he pushed his glasses up his nose and secured me in his arms.

"You can't promise something like that," I muttered into his chest. "You never know what could happen."

But Chris was not in fact dead, and his plane had not in fact blown up. I could finally release the pent-up tension I'd been holding for the past several hours.

"I'm just glad you're okay." Tears and pregnancy hormones and sobs overcame me. "Your plane didn't…"

"Explode? Yeah, thank God for that," Chris filled in for me. "So you heard."

"Only parts of it. What happened?"

Chris guided me to the edge of the bed and we sat down. I crumpled into his lap as he went into the details of the plane fiasco.

"Someone called in an anonymous bomb threat. We ended up having to switch flights, and it was pretty crazy and chaotic. But nothing happened, and I'm here."

"Do they know who did it?"

Chris's body shifted under me. "No, they're still investigating. From what I could gather, they think the threat was made from a burner phone with a Bloodson Bay area code. So it was someone local."

Any hope of this being a coincidence was officially gone. Whoever did it specifically targeted Chris.

"But I don't want you to worry about any of that, because I also have some good news."

Thank you, Lord, I could use some good news.

"I got a job offer."

"You did? That's awesome, babe!"

This meant no relocation, which was the last thing I had wanted to add to my to-do list before bringing a new life into the world.

"It was actually the craziest thing. For starters, it wasn't with the company I had the interview with. It was from a lady I was sitting next to on the plane. We got to talking about my background and experience, and she offered me a job on the spot. Check it out. You're looking at the new data engineer for Bloodson Business Solutions."

He held out his phone, showing me a selfie he had taken on the plane. Beside him sat a woman with hair the color of golden snickerdoodles, toasting for the camera with plastic cups.

Mmm... cookies. The pregnancy cravings were strong tonight.

"So... the job is local, right?" I reiterated.

"Yep, and I'm heading to their office tomorrow to fill out the paperwork and do the final part of the interview. Things are going to be okay, honey. Speaking of which, I assume you kept your promise to take it easy and stay off your feet," Chris reminded me.

Was sitting on your rear behind a Dumpster while a shooter used you for target practice technically *off my feet*?

I wanted to tell my husband about everything going on, but I didn't want to worry him. Especially not right before the most important job interview of his life.

"Of course I took it easy."

But Chris read right through me.

"Tara… you know how at-risk you are being pregnant at your age."

That evoked a scoff.

"My age? What are you saying?" Just because my eggs were more *mature* didn't make me a pregnant invalid.

"You know what I mean. Please lay off the stress. I'm serious when I ask you to take it easy. I'm really excited about the baby, and this might be our last chance. Please, for me, behave."

"I promise."

Shoot. Now I *really* couldn't tell him about getting shot at. But the red sports car down the street. The blonde woman in the photo. And the bomb threat! It all seemed way too coincidental.

"How did you get home, anyway?" I asked, already anticipating his answer.

"Oh, my new boss dropped me off."

Just like I thought.

"She doesn't happen to drive a red sports car, does she?"

"Yeah, a red Dodge Charger. How'd you know?"

Nope, I definitely couldn't tell him what I had been up to the past couple days.

"Just a hunch. I saw the car parked down the street."

He nodded, as if that was totally normal.

"Chris, why is she parked at the end of our street?" I probed.

"She was probably waiting out the storm. Or pulling up navigation directions to get home. How would I know? And why are you so bothered by it?"

He lifted me off of his lap and walked to the bedroom window, peering down the street.

"If she was there, her car's not there anymore, so you can

relax, Tara." He turned back to me, studying me. "Hey, are you worried about this being a scam or something?"

"You could say that."

"I promise you have nothing to worry about. It's totally legit, you'll see."

Maybe I'd just hint at what had been going on. I had never been good at keeping secrets from Chris... which pretty much spoiled every Christmas and birthday and romantic holiday because I couldn't keep my mouth shut.

"I should let you know that Ginger's husband is missing and she has been getting these creepy, threatening notes. I think a blonde woman driving a red sports car might be behind it."

Chris's good mood faded as quickly as a cheap boxed dye job on gray hair. He grabbed me by the shoulders.

"Tara, stop. Just stop! My boss is not behind any threats, and I'm not going to let Ginger's drama risk my new job. Stay out of it!"

"You don't understand, Chr—"

"No, under no circumstance are you to get involved! You're pregnant! Whatever happens to Rick, he got what he deserved. He was a deadbeat dad, a crappy husband, and a criminal."

"But he's important to Ginger," I replied.

"Fine, be a friend to Ginger, but stay out of whatever is going on there. And it wouldn't be a bad idea for Ginger to keep a wide berth from Rick too. Whatever grave Rick dug himself into this time, it's his to die in. He's not taking my wife or her best friend with him."

I went to bed that night relieved that Chris was okay and alive. But if Chris was alive, and the note said that someone's husband was killed, that could only mean that Rick... was already dead.

Chapter 22

The storm outside abated. The thunderclouds cleared out as the morning sun pushed its way in. But the tempest in Ginger's kitchen had only begun.

No amount of morning coffee, or fresh doughnuts, or hugs would pull Ginger out of the funk she was in. When caffeine and sugar didn't work, I knew Ginger was in bad shape.

"Ging, you ready to go?"

Neither of us had been able to reach Sloane, and an ambiguous call to Alika revealed she hadn't spoken to her daughter either. We didn't want to raise any alarm... yet, but it was looking more ominous by the hour.

Ginger shook her head against the inevitable. "What if going to the police makes things worse?"

After the floodwaters receded and the roads cleared, Ginger had promised me we'd go to the BBPD first thing in the morning—twice now!—but clearly I would have to drag her kicking and screaming.

After setting today's *Bloodson Bay Bulletin* newspaper and a fresh *fully-caffeinated* coffee in front of her, I busied myself tidying up the clutter around her kitchen. Across her breakfast nook table Ginger had spread pictures of Rick and Benson, most of them obviously from the 1980s, judging by Rick's neon geometric-patterned sweater and Benson's *Alf* t-shirt. Lifting a stack of pictures, giving each one a long gaze, Ginger seemed to drift back in time further and further with each photograph.

"I keep waiting for it to get easier—losing Bennie without being able to say goodbye. But now Rick… it's like I'm going through it all over again. I didn't even get a last kiss."

She was already referring to Rick in the past tense.

"We don't know for sure that he is…"

For Ginger's sake I didn't finish the sentence. Now I knew just how awful a feeling it was to wonder if it was the last time I was going to see the man I loved. I didn't want to hurt Ginger any more than she was already hurting, even if I did hate the guy for putting my best friend in this position.

"There was blood in the storage unit, Tara. That last note said he was killed. It could only mean one thing. Rick is gone. For good."

With a frown of defeat, Ginger grabbed her purse from the table, sending a bundle of papers to the floor. It was the straw that broke Ginger's back as she suddenly burst into tears.

"Hey, honey, I'll get it. Just sit," I soothed, picking up the mess.

On top was the photo of Benson, the one displayed at his funeral and again on the news at the announcement of his memorial fund. It clearly was Ginger's favorite.

"Do you want me to frame this one for you?" I offered, staring at it.

Ginger's shoulder lifted slightly. "Sure."

Sticking out of a box on the table I found an empty picture frame, about the right size. "Mind if I use this frame?"

Ginger barely glanced at it before her eyes widened.

Reaching out, she grabbed it forcefully out of my hands.

"No, no, not this one," she mumbled, turning the frame over, examining it like it was a puzzle to solve.

In a zombie-like state, she rose from her chair carrying the frame around the table, pushing aside papers and photos, searching for something.

"Ging, do you need help finding something?"

She didn't answer. She just kept rifling through the disarray.

"What are you trying to find?" I asked.

For the first time Ginger seemed to register my presence and blinked once, as if awakening from a dream.

"Oh, nothing. Sorry about that. Sleep deprivation." She blinked again, and then as if someone had swiped away all the cobwebs, her gaze cleared. "What were you saying, dear?"

"I was asking if you wanted me to frame this picture of Benson for you."

Something drew me to the photo, to a specific detail I couldn't quite put my finger on. And then I realized what it was.

"The necklace Benson is wearing here—look at the shape of the gem on it. Doesn't it look a lot like the shape that's missing from Knight Rider's bridle?"

The gem was a pale grayish purple and tacky large. Several carats, easily. I couldn't imagine why any man on earth would wear a piece of jewelry like this, but to each his own, I guess.

It was the unique shape, however, that drew my attention— jagged and almost triangular. Definitely not what you would usually use for a gem setting. Like it was raw and uncut. And not something you'd see in costume jewelry.

"Oh yeah, that does look familiar. Let me find that picture you took of me and Knight Rider." Ginger grabbed her phone and scrolled through her recent photos, finding the one I'd taken of her and the horse at my barn.

She held up her phone to the picture I held, comparing the shapes. "Look—it's a match!"

"I think you've found your missing bridle gem," I said.

"Not exactly. I have no idea where that necklace would be. Probably buried somewhere in this house full of junk."

"Don't worry, we can replace it with something else on the bridle."

Ginger's gaze shifted from the horse photo to Benson. "Do you find it odd that Bennie would have removed a jewel from a bridle and put it on a necklace?"

"Not if it was valuable," I deduced.

"I feel like I've seen it before." Ginger stared at the image of it, her fingertip tapping the picture. "Before Bennie started wearing it. But I can't place why I recognize it. And somehow I know it's, like, super rare or something."

It now made sense why Rick had included the tack with the horse contract—Rick knew the gem's worth. It must have been worth a pretty penny to go through all that trouble.

"But if it's so valuable, why would Rick have embedded it in a horse bridle in the first place, then boarded the horse at Valance Farms where anyone could take it?"

"As Rick always said," Ginger smirked knowingly, "the best place to hide something is in plain sight."

Her gaze returned to the photo, then she set it down and smacked her palm on the table. She was remembering something.

"Wait, I just remembered something! I'm pretty sure Bennie was buried wearing this necklace, along with his matching suit."

Ginger tapped her chin. "If I was a betting woman, I think that whoever is after Rick must be after this stone, and they had to have seen it at Bennie's funeral. That's the only thing that makes sense for why someone would unearth his grave."

"They must not have found it in his casket then, because after they dug him up they kept coming after you. So maybe the gem was stolen by someone else at the funeral."

If the gem was really that valuable, whoever was after it would not give up. We *had* to find it to get the target off Ginger's back.

"Do you remember anyone unusual coming to his funeral?" I asked.

If Ginger could figure out who attended, we would be one step closer to knowing who wanted this gem so darn bad.

"I was too busy grieving to notice who came. Though, there was a sign-in book at the church where people could pay their respects or offer condolences. I'll check that and see if any names stand out."

While Ginger left to search for the funeral attendance book, I snapped a picture of Benson's necklace and did a Google search for what kind of value we were looking at.

The first result that came up was musgravite, what the Gemological Institute of America called "*a rarity among rare*." With less than eight gemstone-quality musgravites mined in the world, it demanded a starting value at $35,000 per carat. But the color purple, a rarer and more desirable color, increased its market value tenfold. This stone was a boulder compared to the size of my humble engagement ring. One of comparable size recently sold for over $800,000.

"Holy guacamole, Ginger. This stone, at this size, is easily worth half a million dollars!" I called to her. "We *really* need to find this sucker!"

"Maybe the funeral director took it off of Bennie and gave it to me. But if he did, I have no idea where I could have put it," Ginger said plainly, seemingly unphased by the sheer magnitude of worth this jewel possessed. "I'll try to look for it, just in case it's somewhere around here," she noncommittedly offered from where I guessed to be her computer room.

She had dubbed it her computer room during the early 2000s, when bulky desktops were still the rage. And according to Ginger and her ancient Pentium computer, they still were. I didn't have the energy to argue that the laptop I had bought her for Christmas last year—which was still in the packaging—was lighter and faster and didn't require her to sit cooped up in that tiny room overflowing with junk.

Technology is the devil, Ginger would tell me. And yet technology could end up saving our lives.

"I know that book is somewhere in here." Ginger's voice was muffled by what I suspected was the floor-to-ceiling clutter. A loud *bang* reached me all the way in the breakfast nook.

"Do you need help in there?" I yelled to her.

"Nope!" she answered, sounding frazzled and buried in junk, but insistent. "It's all good in the hood!"

Embarrassed by her hoard of stuff, Ginger refused to accept help decluttering and cleaning, no matter how much I insisted it was nothing to be ashamed of.

"So I guess our next priority—after finding Sloane—is to find that gem," I repeated, in case Ginger hadn't caught my point.

"Or to tell my stalker to kiss my hairy, flabby butt!" Ginger grunted, followed by an avalanche of *thuds*.

"Your butt is hairy?" I was a little grossed out by the visual.

"The Bible says a woman's hair is her crown." Ginger's voice sounded distant and breathy, like she had been climbing her way out of the avalanche I had just heard.

"I think it was referring to a woman's head, Ging."

When Ginger finally returned to the kitchen, she was carrying a large book that she dropped on the table.

"Ewan Valance was at the funeral," she stated as if the mystery was officially solved.

"And?" I waited for something more. But she gave me nothing.

"And what? He's our culprit."

"Wasn't there anyone else who attended that raises a red flag? We need to dig deeper than just him, because I'm pretty sure he's not our guy. Otherwise he would have noticed the gem in the bridle right away and taken it before Benson had a chance. Whoever wants that jewel dug up Benson's grave. It has to be someone else."

I skimmed the list of names, noticing only a few I didn't recognize. But one stuck out like a pregnant pole-vaulter. I jutted my finger at the name.

"Corbin Roth. He was there." It couldn't be coincidence that his name kept popping up around Rick's disappearance. "It has to be him."

"Do you think all of this—the news clipping threats, the missing gem, Bennie's gravesite getting dug up—is enough evidence to take to the police to get some help finding Rick, if he's alive, and protecting us from Roth?" Ginger was finally thinking the same thing I had been over the past four days.

149

It was time we at least tried.

"So this hideously invaluable gem," I selected a chocolate éclair from the donuts I had brought Ginger, "do you recall anything about how Rick got it?"

The more we knew about its history, the more we could give the police.

Ginger's appetite returned as she joined me in picking out a Boston cream donut for herself. "Yeah, I think I do remember. It was so long ago I had forgotten all about it. To be honest, I had never thought I'd see that jewel again…"

Chapter 23

December 3, 1979

Despite the casualties, The Who concert was groovy, as I had anticipated it would be. But the long drive home, not so much. By the time Rick and I stumbled into our home, my eyes drooped as I headed straight for the bedroom. Rick, on the other hand, was wired after snorting a line of cocaine while on the road, which he didn't realize I had seen. He was ready to go out and party, and I was ready to call him out for lying. Instead I booked it for the bedroom.

"The night is still young, Gingersnap." Rick wrapped his arms around me, moving back and forth like we were in a stilted disco dance. "C'mon, let's go party!"

I shrugged his body off of mine, angry at him over the drugs that I had forbidden him from using. "I don't care what you do, but I'm going to bed. It's been a long day."

I was brushing my teeth when the telephone rang. Rick picked up the mint green receiver after the first ring, said barely a handful of words, then hung it up on the base.

The only calls that came after dark—when proper families were snug as a bug in a rug—had to be an emergency.

"Who the heck is calling at this hour?" I asked, peering around the bathroom door.

"Oh, uh, the boss needs me to come in to work," Rick stammered.

"If you're going to lie, at least make it believable."

"I'm not lying. He has a job for me that could bring in a lot of dough. Fast."

"Fast money is illegal money, Rick."

"We're behind on our mortgage payment, and we could really use the extra cash. It's a quick job. I'll be back in an hour."

Well over an hour came and went before Rick returned home, and I still wasn't asleep as I worried the minutes away. I didn't like these late-night jobs he was taking more frequently, because unless it was a union night job, it couldn't be anything safe... or legal.

Rick found me curled up on the sofa reading *The Hitchhiker's Guide to the Galaxy* wearing my ruffled, apricot floor-length nightgown, while Rick wore a smile I didn't trust.

Nor did I trust him as he dropped to one knee alongside the sofa, pulling something out of his pocket. Tucked inside his closed fist, I couldn't tell what it was as he searched my eyes earnestly.

"Christmas came early this year." Rick's pupils were dilated and his speech rushed, like he was trippin'. "I know I haven't been the best provider, Gingersnap, but I told you one day I'd make it up to you. Today is that day, my foxy mama."

He opened his hand, and inside his palm was a huge purplish-gray jewel. It was hideous and tacky, but Rick seemed too excited and proud of himself for me to say what I really thought.

"Thanks, babe." I picked up the gem, unsure what I was supposed to do with it. It wasn't in a setting, so how was I supposed to wear this bulky thing?

"This here gem is rare. Priceless."

"Where'd it come from?" I asked.

"It's… uh, a family heirloom."

I scoffed.

"What family are you talking about? The Royal Family? Because I know your family doesn't have jewels like this! Unless you're talking about these family jewels—" I reached over and cupped his groin, squeezing a hoot out of him.

"You're missing the point, Ging. We could either sell it and use the cash toward something else, or I could put it in a setting for you and you could wear it."

"You want me to wear… this?" I held it up, only mildly impressed at how the gem caught the dim living room lamp light. "Where'd you get such a valuable stone anyway? And don't feed me no *family heirloom* malarky."

"All I can say is I know someone who knows someone. They asked me to do something and this was my payment."

"Who is this *someone* you're talking about?"

Rick didn't speak, only hung his head.

"It's that Corbin Roth fella, ain't it? I knew it! Jeepers creepers, Rick. You promised me you'd stop working for that putz. He's a criminal!"

I handed the gem back to him, wanting nothing to do with it.

"Return it, please. Clearly you don't know me at all, Rick. I don't care about fancy jewels. What I do care about is *you*— being here and alive and maybe starting a family with me. You really let me down."

That day I hoped to never hear that name Corbin Roth again,

or see that gem again. But as fate would have it, both would come storming back into my life with a vengeance.

Chapter 24

It should have been as simple as $2 + 2 = 4$. After Ginger told me her recollection of the night the gem first appeared, we suspected Corbin Roth hired Rick to acquire this rare and unusual gem, which Rick successfully accomplished. But then he kept it for himself.

Corbin Roth's Gem + Rick Stealing = Certain Death

No one stole from Corbin Roth and got away with it. Not even forty-four years later. And somehow Ginger, Sloane, and I ended up on the receiving end of Corbin's revenge.

There were still some variables in the equation that we hadn't figured out yet, like *who* in Bloodson Bay would have come to possess a half-a-million-dollar jewel in the first place. And *how* did Corbin find out about it?

We hoped to find answers at the Bloodson Bay Police Department precinct.

Apparently Detective Martina Carillo-Hughes didn't agree with my easy math. There was no definitive evidence to tie Corbin to the threats, and this elusive gem was as tangible as a whispered rumor, until someone could substantiate its existence.

A folder dropped from my arm to Detective Hughes's desk, flapping open on impact. Spitting the contents out, the newspaper clippings fanned across her stack of case dossiers. Each clipping headline underlined a different variation of the same threat.

"I thought a picture is worth a thousand words… and enough to prove this gem exists," I explained to the detective while pointing out Benson's picture with the gem hanging from his neck.

"It could be some ugly costume jewelry, for all I know. I can't start an investigation over what could be…" she waved the clippings I had brought, then tossed them on her desk, "senseless pranks, Tara. I can fingerprint these if you want, but if this is coming from a true threat, like you believe, I doubt these will come back with anything."

"What about Sloane? Can you at least start a search for her?" I pushed.

"And don't forget Rick! He's missing too," Ginger cut in emphatically, turning on me with a frustrated glare.

"Are you sure you want me to start digging into this gem and Rick's disappearance, Ms. Mallowan? Because once I start, if it incriminates your husband in any way, you know what that means…"

Ginger had begged me not to tell Marti—I mean *Detective Hughes*, the cop had corrected me in front of Ginger—about the gem in particular yet, since that would incriminate Rick of a pretty big crime if he had stolen it, due to its price tag… God rest his soul, if he was indeed dead. But I honestly couldn't care less. He had brought Ginger nothing but pain and would get the felony he deserved. Or death. I was okay with either one, as long as he and his criminal associates stayed out of my best friend's life.

So I dished it all out to the detective. And I still ended up getting nothing in return.

I had at least thought we could start searching for Sloane. And again, Detective Hughes didn't offer much help.

"I can file the missing persons report and log Sloane Apara's information," Detective Hughes explained, "but we can't launch an official investigation unless our review shows that she could be in danger or we suspect foul play. That review usually requires forty-eight hours in our precinct. That's the best I can do, for now."

Even after I tried to connect the dots for her between the newspaper threats and Sloane's sudden disappearance, the detective couldn't find a connection between Rick and Sloane. For that matter, neither could I.

"Sloane could be taking some personal time, for all you know," the detective suggested, walking Ginger and I down the noisy cubicle-cluttered corridor where dim strip lighting painted everything a sickly pallor.

Several 1990s-era D.A.R.E. posters clung to the end of the wall where the offices exited into the lobby. The ineffective messages were powerless against the reality of rising drug use in our rural town where there wasn't much else to do beside tipping cows and getting into trouble.

"I wish I could be of more help," Detective Hughes concluded, pausing at the exit, "but we don't have the resources to search for a single woman who is known to frequently travel for her job. I'm sure Ms. Apara will turn up, and in the meantime, keep me informed."

An officer approached Detective Hughes, holding the Ewan Valance case file in hand. Ginger took this opportunity to interject herself, talking animatedly with her hands in a whisper I couldn't hear. When Ginger returned, she wore a grin I wasn't sure how to interpret.

"What was that about?" I asked.

"Just greasing the wheels a little," she answered mysteriously. "I had some intel that might help move things along."

Detective Hughes had already retreated halfway down the aisle with the officer when Ginger called after her. "There is one more thing you could help me with, Detective."

Marti halted and turned around, blinking in that slow-motion way that meant we had reached her annoyance threshold.

"Yes, Mrs. Mallowan?"

"Do you know how I'd track down a motorcycle title transfer that happened decades ago?"

Marti thought for a minute, then said, "Do you have the Vehicle Identification Number?"

"Nope."

"Well, then I would suggest you call the DMV and they'll have your entire VIN history and vehicle titles on file. Once you have the VIN, you can do an easy search online for the various owners. I'm sure you can figure it out from there, since you're so keen to play detective." Marti propped her hands on her hips. "Are you happy now?"

Ginger grunted. "Happier than a dead pig in the sunshine."

So we left with no help, and no hope.

Chapter 25

"Not enough resources, my butt!" Ginger grumbled as we drove off. "If they're not keeping innocent civilians like Sloane safe, what are they so busy doing, then?"

That question would momentarily be answered four blocks later as we spotted where these police resources had gone to:

Leonard Valance's house.

Four cop cars—which amounted to most of the Bloodson Bay patrol unit—were parked, lights flashing, out front. Several uniformed officers mulled around the yard, while two others stood sentry next to Leonard near the front door.

"Is that Leonard Valance… in handcuffs?" I wondered aloud.

"That was fast," Ginger muttered. "Pull over! Let's find out."

"And be one of those rubberneckers I hate?" I scoffed as I pulled up to the curb. Of course I wouldn't miss this for the world.

A small knot of housewives had already collected at the edge of the sidewalk, so Ginger and I joined them, blending in. Bound in handcuffs, Leonard was being escorted down his porch steps by one of the officers, and I couldn't help but grin. Finally his life of crime was catching up to him! Maybe this would be the wakeup call that Peace needed.

Oh, shoot. And then there was Peace.

Trailing behind him, tears streaming down her splotchy face, my heartbroken sister-in-law rushed to keep up, sobbing while screaming for the officer to explain the arrest charges.

I overheard one of the cops tell her she could meet her boyfriend at the station and get more information there, while another officer grabbed her by the arm to hold her back from chasing the squad car they were shoving Leonard into.

I watched in horror as my tough-as-nails sister-in-law broke down right then and there. As much as I hated Leonard, I hated seeing Peace distraught even more.

Slipping through the onlookers, I wove my way around the meandering cops and reached out for Peace in a hug. I offered as genuine a consolation as I could muster.

"Peace, what's going on?" I asked. Knowing what I knew, jittery goosebumps spawned over me as I braced for Peace to read me like a book.

"Leo's being arrested for the abduction of Alika Apara, Sloane's mom."

Someone had turned him in. I had expected it would eventually fall on me to do the dirty deed… but I knew I hadn't said anything. So who came forward?

Instantly my spidey-sense woke up.

"Did Leonard tell you that he did it?"

Peace's face contorted in horror. "Of course not! He's innocent. It's probably his psycho father trying to pin what he did on Leo to save his own butt because he knows his son would never turn against him. Especially with the trial coming up."

While I wouldn't put it past Ewan to turn his own son in to

save his skin, I knew it wasn't him this time.

"I've gotta head down to the precinct to see if they'll let me talk to Leo. And I've got to get in touch with a lawyer…" Peace's attention remained fixed on the squad car where her boyfriend sat with the door open while officers stood by talking.

"Do you want me to come with you?" It was an offer I *really* hoped she would decline. I had enough to deal with, but I would go if she needed me there.

"No, I think it's best you not get involved, Tara. But thanks." Peace turned to the house, and I debated whether or not to ask her something that could make things worse.

"Before you go," I blurted out, decision made, "when you talk to Leonard, can you ask him if he had something to do with Sloane disappearing?"

Peace looked over her shoulder cluelessly at me. Apparently Leonard hadn't been honest with her about anything. Then her eyes widened with horror.

I pivoted to see what Peace was gawking at, and standing at Leonard's open police car door was Ginger.

"Did you do something to Sloane?" she screamed, drawing the attention of every officer and looky-loo.

"I didn't do anything!" Leonard insisted. "I swear!"

"Just like you didn't help your father abduct Alika Apara and chain her in a bunker? The truth always catches up to you, Leonard, and you're finally getting what you deserve!"

I would have normally been proud of Ginger for standing up to a Valance, had I not turned around to see Peace's jaw clench and face redden in a mixture of anger, disappointment, and shame. Ginger had gone too far.

My mouth dropped open in a shocked O. "Did you tell the

detective about Leonard?"

"I had to. It could be connected to why Sloane's missing. Everything is relevant… until it isn't."

"I thought we agreed not to tell anyone and let Alika decide what she wanted to divulge."

Ginger shrugged. "That was before our friend disappeared. All bets are off now. I'm so sorry, Peace. I hope you can forgive me."

"You want me to forgive you—" Peace shouted, "for making up lies about Leonard?"

"Ginger isn't lying. Ask Leonard yourself, Peace." I hoped the softness of my tone would reach through to her.

"No… he would never…" Peace lost the words between her tearful sniffles. "Why would you do that to him, Ginger?" Peace's ice-blue gaze cut to my skittish orbs.

"At least I had the balls to stand up to that family!" Ginger defended. "Alika is too terrified of the Valances to tell the cops the truth, and Leonard is too cowardly to confess. So I guess I'm the only one willing to right this wrong and save Sloane."

If it wasn't already too late.

Chapter 26

Peace wouldn't be speaking to me for days, if I was lucky. If I was unlucky, I'd get the silent treatment for months... or maybe even years.

If the history of Peace's ancestors, the founders of Bloodson Bay, had taught me anything, it was that they were extremely gifted in the art of grudges. So severe were these resentments that Peace wrote a book about it back when she was a teenager and it ended up getting published. I made a cameo in her book that I would have preferred to stay out of, but I guess that's what happens when you personally know an author: One way or another you might make it into their books, so better friend than foe. I'd rather be the hero of the story than the villain... or the victim, if the author hated you enough.

After a publicly shamed Leonard was hauled away in the squad car, Peace's stormy stare told me if she wrote another book, I would not be one of the survivors.

The grudge had taken hold.

By the time I got home from the police station, the house was empty. The drapes were drawn, keeping the outside world safely out. Thin strands of light glided in through the fissure, a stirring pink tinged with orange.

I vaguely remembered Chris had somewhere important to

be today. Something that left me feeling deeply unsettled.

I checked my calendar, and the whole day was clear, with the exception of a horse pickup that I had bid on last week at the kill pen auction. The sweetest gelding you'd ever meet, too. A perfect companion for Ginger's Knight Rider, and another reason my husband needed to find a job urgently.

After tossing a quick load of laundry in, I grabbed the stack of clean clothes and began folding and putting them away. Tripping over Chris's open suitcase, I swore to yell at him later about leaving things out when I noticed his nicest suit was missing. That's when it clicked.

Job. Urgently.

Today Chris had that final interview with the woman from his flight home. The snickerdoodle-haired lady who drove a red sports car, just like the one at the storage unit. I didn't know where the meeting was supposed to take place, only that it was at a warehouse being renovated, according to Chris. Renovated… as in vacant. With lots of plastic drop cloths all over… perfect for easy cleaning of the blood spatter. Sure, *that* didn't sound ominous.

Despite Chris's insistence that it was completely legit, he didn't know the half of what had happened while he was gone. An impromptu job offer in the Bloodson Bay drug district sounded sketchy as it was, but her car matching the exact description of our shooter?

I couldn't help but check on him, in case he was walking into danger. But this time I would be packin' heat.

Luckily we both fervently believed in keeping our phone tracking on, ever since we found a dead body buried in our yard. As long as Chris had cell service, it should have been easy to find him.

Opening the tracking app, I found Ginger's icon safely tucked away next door and Chris's pinned location on the outskirts of town, what locals called the G-Spot. And get your mind out of the gutter, because no, it was not what you're thinking. G stood for Grave, as in Grave Spot, because too many bodies had been found on that side of Bloodson Bay due to heavy drug trafficking.

Speaking of which, fifteen minutes later I passed at least three drug deals going down as I drove into the heart of the G-Spot, eventually pulling into a huge empty lot in front of a rundown warehouse. The facility looked like it may have been useful forty years ago as a manufacturing plant, but it had since fallen into rot and decay, with nearly every window broken, bricks covered in ivy, and the rancid smell of garbage permeating the air. This looked like the perfect place to murder someone and dump a body.

Double-checking Chris's location, his little icon hadn't moved so I drove around the back, praying it was the right spot… no pun intended. When I saw his car parked next to a red sports car, my adrenalin pulsed and heart quickened.

The gun's handle nearly slipped out of my sweaty palm as I snuck up to the building's entrance. Stealthily making my way to the rusted metal door that hung crookedly on its sliding hinges, I crept inside the warehouse, hearing the echo of a woman's voice somewhere within.

Natural light was a scarce in this high-ceilinged space, creating a gloom full of shadows. At the far corner, brightness poured out of a sliver of open door where there appeared to be an office. I tiptoed my way toward it, then swung the door open, gun cocked and aimed.

"Tara!" Chris sputtered, both shocked and mortified.

He jumped up from where he was sitting in a chair across from the woman whose picture he had shown me. She scooted back, screaming with her hands up.

It appeared to be exactly what Chris had said it was: an interview. The woman was dressed in a pantsuit, and a neat stack of papers sat on the desk between them. A quick glance at the wording confirmed it was contractual legalese. I lowered the gun.

"Uh... hi?" I stammered.

I didn't know what to say or how to remedy this. I had really messed up. And most certainly cost Chris his ideal job by scaring the piss out of his future boss.

"Forgive my wife, Elena. She's a little paranoid after everything that happened with the bomb threat on the plane yesterday," Chris explained, trying to diffuse the situation and secure his job offer. "Elena, meet Tara. Tara, meet my new boss Elena... as long as I still have the job offer."

Elena laughed good-naturedly, a sweet sound to my ears. "I can't fault a modern woman for being brave enough to rescue her man... even if he's no longer in danger. It's nice to meet you, Tara."

"I am so so sorry," I gushed.

"It happens," Elena assured me.

"Does it, though?" I chuckled with embarrassment. I was pretty sure wives didn't barge in all SWAT team in the middle of their husband's job interviews. "I just have to say I love your car."

"Oh, that?" Elena glanced out the only window that

166

appeared to be intact in the whole building. "That's not mine. It's a rental I picked up last night at the airport."

Now *that* put a dent in my theory. A good dent that meant Chris's job was legit, but a bad dent because our shooter was still at large.

WHAT SHE DOESN'T KNOW

Part 3
Sloane Apara

WHAT SHE DOESN'T KNOW

Chapter 27

When I awoke, the panic seeped in slowly rather than in a burst, cold and heavy and… dark. So dark, as if light had been locked away for an eternity.

I couldn't feel the silk head wrap I usually slept in that bound my curls at night. I didn't smell the creamy coconut oil I lathered on my body before bed. And I most certainly noticed the lack of morning sun usually pouring through my floor-to-ceiling bedroom windows.

Instead I felt the rough texture of burlap against my cheek. Smelled the pungent scent of men's over-doused cologne. And saw absolute darkness.

I was lying down, but I wasn't in my bed. In fact, I didn't remember ever going to bed. I didn't know how I had gotten here—wherever *here* was. Or what bound my arms and legs in an awkward backward pretzel. Or why my skull throbbed as if it had been split wide open.

Time slipped like sand through my fingers, a steady stream of missing minutes I couldn't hold. As the hazy details of yesterday—was it yesterday? or was I out for longer?—congealed into a vague memory, I recalled the flash of the doorbell light blinking throughout the house, then stepping out into the evening gray to find a package on my porch.

The package.

The memory slowly hardened into a crisp visual…

I hadn't seen who might have left the package, not a car or person in sight. But my long driveway obscured the rod, and dense live oaks surrounded my house, easily obstructing even the most conspicuous of hiders. I was too distracted by the unmarked cardboard box to pursue a search of the perimeter anyway, because this didn't belong on my porch. I suspected what it was, what I'd find inside, and it should not be here, could not be mine.

I opened it anyway.

Upon opening the package, I unfolded a newspaper clipping, similar to the ones Ginger had received. I guessed as much the moment I saw the box. The oddity of it being delivered to my house struck me instantly, until I remembered that Tara was supposed to meet me here tonight for a Feel the Noize Party Planning meeting to discuss the children's home fall fundraiser. Still, these messages were for Ginger, not for me or Tara. So why was it left at my home?

Feeling around in my memory a little deeper, there was something else. But what? The details were just out of reach.

My phone. Which I felt the absence of in my back pocket where I usually kept it. I couldn't recall what happened to the phone after I texted Ginger about the package, asking her to come over to read the underlined message. She had responded, telling me she would be on her way. Had she come? Was she bound in here beside me?

Although my hands were tied behind my back, I stretched my legs out until they met a hard surface. A car back seat most likely, I discovered as my shoes kicked the other car door. If

172

Ginger wasn't in the back seat with me, had she been thrown in the trunk?

The text exchange brought my memory to a dead end. After that I remembered… nothing.

As I turned on my side, a sharp thrum of pain shot across the back of my head, where I felt a growing bump. Wriggling my arms and legs was futile, as they were tied together tightly with what I assumed was duct tape. It was too slick and sticky to be rope.

My headache spread from temple to temple, but the worst of it split the back of my skull in two. The hair felt matted, and my scalp felt damp. Most likely blood.

I must have gotten knocked out with a sharp blow to the head. After that, the minutes, hours, days were all nonexistent. Now here I was—except I didn't know where *here* was. Or how I, of all people, managed to end up in this position.

I was diligent. Lacking one of my five senses—hearing—had made me this way from the very beginning. As if the other four senses—sight, touch, taste, and smell—elevated themselves in order to make up for their lost sibling. So naturally I always noticed what lurked in the shadows, smelled the storms coming, felt the presence of another, and tasted when something wasn't prepared right. At what point had I let my guard down? I couldn't remember.

Did I not notice a strange taste in the mint tea I sipped? Had I overlooked the shifting of strange shadows in my home? Could I have mistaken the smell of an unfamiliar man's cologne for a new candle I had lit?

The bumping of my "prison" indicated I was in a moving vehicle, and based on the soft leather beneath the few patches of my exposed skin, a luxury car. But with the burlap sack over my head, I couldn't see, or barely breathe. It was suffocating—both in reality and in my head.

Death itself didn't frighten me. Whoever had captured me couldn't scare me with threats of ending this shadow life when something better waited on the other side. Like my baba. The art of dying, however, at someone else's whim gripped me so tightly it hurt.

This moment—this completely dark moment—was my singular nightmare. Not only was I unable to hear the threat coming, but I was unable to see it as well.

Chapter 28

The nightmare only got worse.

We hadn't been driving long before the vehicle slammed to a stop, throwing me to a carpeted, cramped floor as I rolled off the seat. With disoriented, limited movements I pushed myself into a sitting position, huddling against the door, squished between the front and back seat.

Suddenly the door behind me disappeared and I fell backward, swiftly slamming my shoulder and head against the concrete below. I hung halfway out of the car, upside down, unable to right myself with my arms bound behind my back.

A waft of wind slid under the edge of the burlap sack over my head, and a pair of rough hands clenched my forearms with a vice grip, yanking me upright to my feet.

Mummy came to mind, and I wondered if this was what it had been like for her on that fateful October in 1995. Had her abductor roughed her up first? Did he deprive her of all her senses? Did fear chew at her bones the same way it did mine? Did she wonder if this would be her last conclusive memory of a life cut short?

The cologne I had detected in the car smelled more pungent as I was dragged closer to my kidnapper—a man, based on the size of his hands and spicey cedarwood smell of him—as he hauled me across a slick, smooth floor. Not a rough concrete outdoor driveway, like I had thought, but smooth like tile. A floor you might find in a garage. The faint scent of gasoline confirmed my guess.

I stumbled beside my captor as he led me up a step and into another dwelling. Instant lemony, crisp, clean air. It had to be his home. A big one, based on the sheer length of it as we walked and I counted my steps.

He guided me down a set of stairs, causing me to nearly fall forward as my feet hadn't adjusted to the first step's drop. Eventually we made it to the bottom, where I shuffled beside him to a chair that he sat me in. The seat was rigid with a ramrod straight back, immobile as if bolted to the floor. A most uncomfortable seat, second to the wooden pews Mummy and I sat in every Sunday at church.

Only now, after blindly maneuvering through the obstacle course of his home, did he finally remove the burlap sack from my head. An unnatural light caused my eyes to wince and tear up. When my vision finally adjusted to the overhead basement lighting, I looked face-to-face at a crooked-nosed man with a crooked smile—a dark, evil man with looks to match.

"Nighty-night," I thought I read on his lips.

I didn't understand. "Huh?"

The question was mixed with the decision that he would be the second man I would have to kill in my life.

But killing him would have to wait, because a moment later I felt a pinch on my arm as he shoved a needle into my vein, and the world began drifting. I sensed him leaving me to journey alone into the dark landscape of barbed dreams.

Chapter 29

If this scenario had been a horror movie, Tara would have predicted that I wouldn't make it out alive. But I wasn't the slutty hot girl, or the Black comic relief character. I was a final girl, and I was too smart to let some ignorant villain outsmart me or kill me. Even if he did have the upper hand.

For now.

When I awoke a second time, I didn't know how many hours had passed. It wasn't long enough that my stomach felt ravenous, or my bladder ached for release. So my best guess was that mere hours had passed since the time he had first knocked me out.

I had barely been conscious a few minutes—not long enough to get a feel for my surroundings—when the crooked-nosed man appeared at the end of a long room carrying something. Only when he was a few feet away did I see what it was.

A knife. Which he then proceeded to press against my throat. The smooth blade pinched my skin in a warning that swallowing a little too hard could slice open my jugular.

"You're finally awake, Sloane Apara. Do you know why I brought you here?" I read from his crooked lips.

I could immediately tell he hadn't done his homework on

me. The way he spoke, lips barely moving, he didn't know I was Deaf, which meant he also didn't know I could read lips. Which some might find to be a disadvantage, but for me it was exactly what I needed to survive.

Nor did he know my history. The Nigerian roots from my mummy's side sparked a fire deep within my belly. Although born and raised in America, I had spent time in my home country as a strong-willed teenager in the 1990s, during one of the worst years of political and economic instability. I lived firsthand under the iron fist of military rule, and watched my own family be exiled as the Niger Delta conflict drove the people into extreme poverty. Those dark days, that survivor's instinct, forged a strength in me that now resurfaced.

"I don't understand you. I'm Deaf," I spoke, knowing my voice would be a clear giveaway.

He looked confused, then aghast, as if deafness was contagious.

"What did you say?" His lip curled as he spoke, making it hard to decipher.

"Write." I kept it one-word simple for him.

While most people understood me when I spoke, thanks to years of speech therapy with my mummy, I purposefully exaggerated the sounds to make it harder for him to understand. I wasn't going to make getting information from me easy.

It looked like he wasn't going to fall for my trick, until he got up and left, returning a few moments later with a roll of duct tape, a pen, and a notepad. Perfect. Almost. Except for the extra duct tape.

"We can't let you run off now, can we?"

He wrapped the duct tape around my legs, securing them to

the chair. Then he scribbled something down, turning the paper toward me to read it:

You have something of mine and I want it back.

I shook my head, nodding toward the pen and paper, then I wriggled my hands so he would notice my bindings.

No, I can't free your hands.

He showed me his reply to my nonverbal request, but until he freed my hands, he wouldn't get what he wanted… and I couldn't get what I wanted. I shrugged, closed my eyes, and leaned back, making sure he knew we were at a stalemate.

I could feel his breath and the vibrations of the air as he spoke—probably cussing me out. Then he yanked my wrists, startling my eyes open. Securing the knife back against my throat, he tapped the pen against a new sentence he had written:

Try to escape and I will gut you like a pig. Oink oink.

I shifted away from the knife's edge and nodded warily in agreement.

Using the dagger, he sliced off the duct tape from my wrists, which left a sticky residue over my skin along with a red rash. I rubbed my sore flesh to recirculate the blood flow that had been slowed by the tight bindings.

Where are you hiding the gem?

I didn't know what gem he referred to, but I couldn't show my cards too soon. I needed to get him talking. Comfortable. Unsuspecting.

Which gem are you talking about?

I wrote back, my hand trembling as he adjusted the blade against my neck. Then he scribbled a reply that would make this situation almost impossible to get out of:

The one worth a million dollars that I won't hesitate to kill you over.

A million-dollar gem? Was he crazy? I would think I'd know if I owned something of that value, and I definitely didn't wear jewelry worth that kind of money.

I would be the first to admit I was slightly high-maintenance, with my nail salon manicures and couture outfits and high-end vehicle that I paid cash for. But even I had the sense to budget and stick to a reasonable price tag.

He seemed convinced I possessed this priceless jewel, but no matter what I said, he'd have to kill me. I was a loose end either way. Even though he had the wrong woman, he clearly he wasn't going to let me plead my case. But I'd be dead if I didn't try:

I don't own anything like that. Whoever pointed you to me clearly doesn't have all the facts. Or they lied to you.

He snickered in my face, grossing me out with his spittle spraying my cheek. Then he wrote something that left me feeling both baffled and betrayed:

It looks like you're the one who doesn't have all the facts— about your own family. I'm talking about the gem your friend killed your father over.

Chapter 30

...the gem your friend killed your father over.

As I read the words on the paper, I refused to believe the Crooked Man. He was lying, because there was no way any friend of mine would betray me with lies, let alone hurt my family.

Then again, my father's death remained an unsolved mystery, and this man seemed to know something about it. Unless it was a manipulation tactic. But for what gain?

I would give him one last shot to deescalate this, one more chance to explain himself before I killed him. I had done it once before, and I would do it again:

I don't know what gem you're talking about, but my friends would never do that. You've got the wrong family. But if you let me go now, we can agree it was a terrible misunderstanding and I won't turn you in to the police.

The blade crowded my throat while he used his free hand to pull out his phone and show me a picture. It was the photo Ginger and I had agreed on using for Benson's memorial.

The Crooked Man pointed to the necklace peeking out from beneath my ex-husband's gray suit that I had specially tailored for him back when we were married, for an overpriced ego-boosting event honoring a bunch of rich, white men. Now my ex was buried in the suit… along with the gem.

I glanced at the picture, then up at the Crooked Man.

"Gem," he stated, his lips exaggerating the word.

Then he returned to the notepad:

Benson was buried with this necklace on. I saw it at the funeral. But when I dug him up it was gone.

So this was the creep who messed with Benson's grave. At least we now knew who was behind it and why. But I still didn't understand why I was bound to this chair.

What does this have to do with me?

He took a long time to reply, so long that I knew it would be a revelation that would destroy me with its truth:

Ginger stole it from your father. She is the reason he's dead.

My father owned a million-dollar gem that Mummy had never once mentioned? No. I didn't understand the connection between my father's death and a gem I had never laid eyes on in my entire life, nor did I care why Ginger stole it—if she actually did. I didn't care about some ugly piece of jewelry. All I wanted was to find a way out of here.

Based on the descending stairs, along with the lack of windows and natural light, I had assumed we were in a basement. A huge one. The air held a slight musty scent, but it was pristine and well decorated, with the exception of this concrete-hard chair that my legs were still bound to.

If I figured out a way to dodge the knife taunting my throat, I needed to plot the fastest way out of here, which would involve first finding the stairs in this labyrinthian space.

A movie-theatre size television hung on the wall in the middle of the room, surrounded by lush leather recliners. On the other end a pool table sat beneath a long, stained-glass billiard light. Definitely not an *Amityville Horror* kind of creepy basement, but a portal to a different kind of hell, nonetheless.

The room stretched in both directions beside me, so it was a gamble which way would lead to the stairs out of here, and which would lead to a dead end. Literally.

He was waiting for my reaction. I finally gave him one, the only one I had:

I don't know anything about it.

A strange contorted grin lifted his lips as he wrote:

You better be sure, because I'm going after your mother next.

I yanked the notepad from him and scribbled frantically:

What does my mother have to do with it? Leave her out of it!

He laughed. "You don't know?"

I looked at him, trying to figure out if this was some game meant to control me, or if there was truth buried under there somewhere.

I watched as a terrible story unfolded on the paper before me, one that involved my dead father and my best friend in a horrible, twisted connection:

Your father's death wasn't an accident. He was murdered,

and your friend is to blame.

Chapter 31

A flimsy curtain separated the past from the present, coexisting in my mind as I sat in a wealthy man's torture chamber, forced to relive the details of my father's murder.

The police had never found my baba's killer, so Mummy had never gotten closure. The only details she had been told—and thus the only details that trickled down to me—were that my father had been the victim of a simple robbery gone wrong. Stabbed, comatose for over a year, then dead, leaving Mummy a widowed mother of a newborn, all for $32 cash.

At least that's what the police told Mummy back then. And we believed it for decades.

Baba's wallet had been taken, the dollar bills of which were missing when the police found it tossed in an alley days after his attack. The facts corroborated their theory, but underneath that story was a thick layer none of us had known about.

Shock filled me as the Crooked Man explained how Baba was in possession of a gem many years ago—back in 1979, before I was born, after he brought Mummy from Nigeria to live in the United States.

Although I had never met my baba, Mummy had told me with pride how Baba worked for Doctors Without Borders, which is how they met when he brought medical supplies to her

Nigerian tribe back in the 1970s. While treating Mummy's malaria, Baba fell in love with her, despite the interracial controversy that attempted to tear them apart.

Out of respect for their conservative family and traditions, my grandfather demanded Mummy keep her Nigerian last name, but that didn't deter Baba from marrying her. Too poor to afford a proper ring, as was customary in America, he vowed to prove his worth to the Apara family after he finished his obligation to Doctors Without Borders.

He left for Australia, then returned with something more valuable than anyone could imagine.

During one of his last missions to the Outback, he saved an Aboriginal woman's life, so the husband thanked my baba with a gift—a rare gem only found in the rural Australian bush. Giving this gem to Mummy, her family approved of their union and off to America my parents went.

Only, for years they never knew the gem's true worth. Until my baba made a deadly mistake.

The Crooked Man filled in some blanks I had never heard before. How Baba took the rare gem to get appraised by a local jeweler, which put a target on Baba's back. The jeweler, full of greed, discovered it was worth a fortune and passed this information on to the Crooked Man, hoping they could negotiate a deal to split the profits once they fenced the gem. This deal would end in my baba's death.

The Crooked Man hired someone to steal the gem, but when the thief returned empty-handed, a story unfolded that my baba fought back and ended up stabbed, and soon the police were on their way. The thief fled, unable to retrieve the jewel.

So the lie went.

Until the Crooked Man stumbled over the truth.

I only knew the very last part—how Baba remained in a coma for over a year, while Mummy birthed me all alone in a foreign land with no family to support her. I came into this world without a father, and my mummy came into motherhood without a husband.

What neither the Crooked Man nor I could figure out was how Benson ended up with the gem. Had my then-husband stolen it from my mother? The Crooked Man had assumed as much when he saw the memorial picture on the news of Benson wearing the gem last year, with my photo next to his.

When he once again saw the necklace on Benson at the funeral, he devised a plot to unearth the body and retrieve the gem. This took time, however, as finding a willing excavator to dig up a dead body in a public cemetery proved difficult.

Even digging up the body proved futile. The gem had been moved… again. The only logical assumption was that it had been returned to the original owner: my mummy. But with Mummy tucked safely away at an undisclosed location, I became the next target.

And so here we were.

This revelation was a tornado, fierce and unsteady and destructive. As my captor uncovered the macabre details surrounding my father's plotted murder, I didn't give a damn about the priceless value of the gem. Or that someone had removed it from Benson's body. Only one nagging thought dawdled at the end of my fingertips:

Who did you hire to kill my father?

Crooked Man rose from his seat, relaxing his arm as he shook his head.

"Wow, I really thought you knew. I was surprised when you married Benson Mallowan, but now I see why. You didn't know."

Then he stooped down to write one last line:

You married the son of your father's killer.

Chapter 32

Everything felt numb. The threat to kill my captor didn't pulsate in my hands anymore, but it was still vibrating somewhere. The urge would return… after I got what I needed to know.

"Are you saying that Rick Mallowan killed my baba?" The words slipped out before I could rally them back in.

I hadn't intended on letting my kidnapper affect me with his lies, but this was no lie. That much was clear on his face.

"I don't know what a *baba* is," he scoffed, and I wanted to smash his smug face in while I educated him on the Nigerian word for *father*. "But yeah, you can thank your ex-husband's father—or should I say your best friend's husband?—for your dad's death."

The Crooked Man knew about my friendship with Ginger. I wondered how long he had been investigating us, digging into my life.

There were too many potholes in the story, big enough to disappear in. Had my own ex-husband known about the gem's origins? Did my best friend? Had they been keeping Rick's secret from the police, from *me*, refusing to give my mummy the closure she deserved? Even now Ginger continued to protect Rick, all for the sake of love, then asked me to help *save* my own father's killer!

I assumed Rick was somewhere in this very same basement. It didn't make sense why Crooked Man asked *me* where the gem was instead of asking Rick himself, so I asked exactly that:

Why not ask Rick where the gem is?

Seconds passed. Several of them. Each one punctuated by the tick of the man's pen against the note pad in a steady beat. Then he wrote a single word that opened this case wide open:

Disappeared.

If the Crooked Man wasn't behind Rick falling off the grid, who was?

"He's as slippery as a fish," he spoke. "And he'll be swimming with them if I ever find him," I read from his lips. "A bad guy like Rick in love with a good girl like Ginger is a ticking time bomb, and I don't want to be near that explosion. It makes him unpredictable and stupid. Stupid enough to steal a valuable gem from me and hide it from me all these years. But I'll win in the end. I always do."

Not this time, I vowed.

"Here's the deal. I'll let you live if you tell me where Rick is."

I was tempted to tell him where he could at least find a clue to Rick's whereabouts—the storage unit. But as much as I wanted Rick to suffer for what he did to my baba, I wanted to help the Crooked Man even less. So I instead told him where he could stick his question—up his butt.

He snarled. "Then I guess that makes you useless to me."

His mouth drooped at an exaggerated angle as our long interrogation gathered around his puffy, red eyes. After consulting the floor, he jotted down one last note, readjusted the knife's tip under my chin, then dropped the pen and notepad on my lap:

It's time to end this. If you tell me where the gem is, I'll set you free. If you don't, consider these your last rites.

He thought his scare tactics would make me crumble. I had watched Nigerian journalists expose the darkest government corruption, their words more powerful than any militia threat. They had inspired a truth in me back then that I still carried with me today: indeed, the pen was mightier than the sword.

I fisted the pen, then swung my arm out, jutting the ballpoint tip directly into his oily red eyeball.

While he was momentarily blinded, I yanked the knife from his weakened grip and stab-stab-stabbed him in the gut until he stood up and reeled backward out of reach.

My legs were still bound to the feet of the chair, so I sawed across the duct tape, the process taking longer than I had expected to break through several layers.

Just as I freed my legs, he lunged toward me, grabbing for

the knife. With one last shove I plunged the entire dagger into his side, but it was too deep to pull back out as his flesh suctioned around the blade.

Four lethal stabs to the torso and a pen sticking out of his eyeball should have brought him to his knees, but this demon-man was still standing!

I jumped up, wondering which way to go. Toward my left I noticed a set of car keys sitting on a table. Presumably he'd dropped them off on his way into the room, so I ran toward the keys, grabbed them, and hoped the stairs were around the corner.

They were, but also around the corner was my abductor, who had miraculously managed to pull the knife out of his side and circle around the other side of the basement. Leaping up the stairwell, I took the steps several at a time as he scrambled after me, chasing my heels with a supernatural endurance. As my foot landed on the top step, he grabbed hold of my ankle and pulled, nearly toppling me backward.

Grabbing the railing, I kicked back with my free foot, landing a heel to his jaw that was jarring enough to break his grip. I slammed the basement door shut as I sprinted through, searching for a way out of this monstrosity of a house.

I recalled mentally counting the number of steps we had taken from the garage to the basement, in preparation for this very moment. So I backtracked as best as my sensory-deprived memory served. The first door I came to felt about right, which led me down a step and into the garage and its familiar gasoline smell. I closed the door behind me, hoping it hadn't made a sound that would guide my captor this way.

Three cars sat in a row. I didn't have time to try each one

with the Crooked Man about to burst through the door at any moment. With a press of the alarm I was able to find the blinking lights of the car quickly. I sprinted toward it, unlocking it as I ran. I had just given my location away.

Settling into the seat, I started the engine and searched for a garage door button. But I was taking too long. There were too many buttons.

A body flung across the windshield, scaring me into action. When a crack splintered across the glass, I noticed a hammer in his hand. Raising his arm again, he dropped it hard in an explosive burst. Another swing, another fissure, then another and another. This psycho was hanging on the car, breaking his way inside. There was no time for opening garage doors.

I shifted the car into reverse, hit the gas, and felt the jarring crunch as I blasted through the glass and chrome garage door. Shards of metal flew around the car like a sharp cape as I careened backwards down the driveway, eventually slamming to a stop. Spinning the steering wheel, I threw the car into drive, bumping across the grassy lawn and thudding over a row of bushes.

When I finally met the asphalt road, the Crooked Man had managed to chase me halfway down the driveway. Nothing would seem to kill him.

I knew then this wasn't over.

WHAT SHE DOESN'T KNOW

Part 4
Ginger

WHAT SHE DOESN'T KNOW

Chapter 33

Sometimes I missed being the chaotic redheaded little girl with cinnamon bark freckles. But there were perks to being an eighties-lovin' old lady with steel-wool hair and an affection for red lipstick. At a certain age, you inherit certain freedoms. The freedom to wear plaids with florals. The liberty to use the handicapped parking spot, even if the cane is just for show. The choice to blurt out whatever comes to mind, then blame it on dementia.

No one scolds you, except your companions and clinicians. And no one notices you when you walk onto a crime scene and poke around.

It had been another sleepless night worrying about Sloane. And worrying about Sloane made me worry about Rick. Was he safe? Scared? Hurt? As tough-guy as Rick could act on the outside, he was a softie at heart. I'd seen him cry over the Sarah McLachlan animal shelter commercial more than once.

I would catch a glimpse of him teary-eyed, and any resentment inside me would soften into forgiveness for whatever wrong he had committed this time. There was no caging the love or despair, as they were tangled in a singular knot I could never unravel.

After a night that crawled at a snail's pace, I checked the

bathroom cabinet, hoping for sleepy-pill relief with Rick's prescription Xanax. They weren't where they usually were. Giving up, I started a pot of coffee and got dressed. As the dawn cracked open to the day, my joints cracked awake along with it.

I checked my email to see if the DMV had found the name on the motorcycle transfer that Rick had gotten pummeled over back in 1977. Last night I had given an over-descriptive white-lie explanation to a nice customer service gentleman, saying that my only deathbed wish—after a long battle with Mad Cow Disease—was to be reunited with that long-lost motorcycle. With only mild hesitation he offered to dig up the bike's entire title history.

"Anything to help a dying lady's dream come true," he had told me. I supplied my email address, and he supplied his home phone number... *"just in case you need anything. I hear Mad Cow Disease can be brutal."* The only thing I needed was a priest and a confessional.

Now I was in my car driving and deliberating, deliberating and driving, then driving to distract myself from deliberating. It was before day had risen, when the night still clung to the corners. I found myself heading into the parking lot of Luna's Restaurant.

My mind slipped easily over to Gunther, wondering if he would be bartending later today, then I yanked those naughty thoughts back. There was no room for ordinary Gunthers in my messed-up crazy Rick drama, no matter how much both men jostled for the lead in my heart.

Luna's was closed, naturally, at this early hour, which made what I saw that much more alarming.

Apparently I wasn't the only one with messed-up crazy

drama. The red lights of an ambulance blinked across the brown windows of the restaurant, along with red-and-blue strobes from two police cars. An officer rolled out yellow caution tape across the door, and I spotted Detective Hughes ushering looky-loos, still dressed in bathrobes and pajamas, to the sidewalk for interviews.

I parked, wondering what had happened, because not every death got the BBPD royal treatment. If Detective Martina Carillo-Hughes was investigating, this wasn't some accident. It was murder.

Suddenly Gunther returned to mind, and I searched the small but growing crowd for him. With no sign of him, I'd be sure to watch the news when I got home later. Or maybe stop by later to check on him in person.

An EMT wheeled a gurney out the front door toward the ambulance, the body bag zipped up. Such a shame to die that way—in public. I wondered if whoever it was even got a chance to finish eating first. Though what was Luna's Steak and Seafood serving at this early hour?

A big dish of homicide, that's what!

I didn't think about my own death often, but when I did, I hoped I went peacefully in private. I heard your bowels released upon death, and I certainly didn't want neighbors and friends watching me crap my pants—alive or dead. I did enough embarrassing stuff in my lifetime; I deserved to go out with the little dignity I had left.

Distracted by the scene behind me, I was heading out of the parking lot when I nearly rammed into a parked car: red and sporty. I slammed on the break and pulled up beside it, looking for the make and model.

I recognized the Chevrolet emblem, but no model was evident on the tail. I got out of my car and walked around the vehicle, my not-yet-warmed-up knees cracking like a pellet gun. Along the side I saw the silver name of the model contrasting against the red paint: Camaro.

It looked just like the car at Stow Away, Don't Throw Away.

Had our shooter struck again, the poor victim draped in that plastic body bag? It would seem that this deadly pool was growing, and there was no escape for any of us.

Chapter 34

I was sitting on the toilet when I heard the front door slam shut.

"Rick?" I yelled with strained hope.

I knew it wouldn't be so easy as him just waltzing through the door like we were a normal family on a Saturday morning and my sweetie-pie was surprising me with fresh-baked croissants.

There was no answer other than a lingering breeze that wandered through the house, fluttering the dangling roll of toilet paper.

"Tara, is that you?" I called out more confidently.

Again, more silence. Until a long, dull scrape tore through the quiet.

My heart stopped, a pause in place of a beat, as fear filled me so fast I grew dizzy.

"Hello?" I meant to yell, but it came out a whisper.

I wondered if perhaps I had misheard. Maybe it wasn't the door slamming at all. Or something scraping the floorboard. How often had Rick accused my overactive imagination of conjuring up unlikely scenarios when he would come home late?

Lately it seemed like I would either hear things that weren't there, or not hear things that were. Like the umpteen times I'd

203

ask Tara to repeat herself because she mumbled—even though she insisted it wasn't her muttering, rather I needed hearing aids. Though lately I *was* relying more on my hands than on my ears to communicate. It was as if my ears hadn't decided yet if they were ready to give up or not.

Just as I had finally convinced myself that indeed my ears had a mind of their own, I heard the unmistakable bang of a cabinet door closing. Followed by a dull rush of water.

"Who's there?" I announced, realizing only after the fact that if it was the shooter coming to finish the job, I had just told them where they could find and kill me. Half-naked in the bathroom, of all places.

I thought crapping my pants was a bad way to die? Getting shot while on the toilet—wearing my ugliest-patterned grannie panties, to boot—was by far the worst way to go. After I quickly finished up, I huddled down near the bathroom tile floor, noticing a layer of grime around the baseboard that I really needed to deep clean one of these days.

My knees popped in angst, my hip bones cracked in annoyance. I creaked open the bathroom door to peer down the hall. Unable to see into the kitchen from here, I figured if I ran fast enough and stealthy enough, I could make a dash for the front door without being seen or heard. Especially if my intruder had unreliable ears like mine.

The kettle began to shrill. Panic began to set in. With my head down, I shuffled, popping and cracking, all the way to the sofa before I ran headfirst into a pair of legs. Blood covered the front of them, and my body froze.

Sugar, honey, iced tea! (A phrase my Irish *mamó* used instead of the cuss word that her ultra-religious upbringing forbid.)

With a slow gaze upward, I nearly choked on the surprise. I should have known that criminals didn't serve tea before killing you.

"Sloane!" I popped up—take *that*, bad knees!—and grabbed her in a hug, smearing blood all over the front of my Prince *Purple Rain* t-shirt. A spritz of peroxide would get that out, I assured myself. As for the blood on Sloane, we'd need a whole bottle.

"Are you hurt?" I asked, searching her up and down for the wound.

"It's okay. I'm okay." She shook her hand at me to stop. "Don't worry, that's not my blood."

That didn't necessarily make me feel any better, though. "Dare I ask whose blood it is?"

"Well, it's a long story…"

"I have nothing but time and tea. Tara and I were worried sick about you! Where have you been? We thought you were kidnapped."

"I *was* kidnapped," she signed. "But I escaped and couldn't go home, and I didn't have my cell phone to call 9-1-1. I think I dropped it on my porch, and I was afraid he might have sent someone to my house to kill me… if he's still alive… so I came here first."

"Based on the amount of blood you're wearing, you must have gotten him good."

"Let's hope it was good enough to put a stop to him. Permanently."

I could feel my face contort in horror, which I hoped didn't offend Sloane. Maiming another human was one thing… but taking it one huge leap further, to the point of no return? I had watched firsthand as a live person became a dead corpse, but being the one to do it required some serious therapy.

"Are you going to be okay," I ventured, "if he's… dead?"

Sloane glanced away, ashamed. When she dared another look at me, she softened with a secret. "I need to share with you a little piece of my past that may help you understand me better. But you may think differently of me after I tell you."

I placed a hand on her shoulder. "I would never think differently of you, Sloane."

She shook her head. "You will, Ginger, and that's okay. It's not an easy thing to confess, but it's part of me now. And always will be."

"Okay," I encouraged.

By now the tea kettle was in the middle of a hissy fit, so I gestured her to follow me to the kitchen. Sloane had already set out two mugs on the counter with tea bag tags hanging over the sides of each. I poured us each a cup and assessed the cluttered counter. Looking around, I realized I was starting to wander into hoarder status. The amount of *stuff* everywhere was bordering on illness.

I pushed a stack of photos toward one end of the breakfast nook table, the domino effect nearly knocking over a small vase of pink carnations. Once I had cleared off a space for our tea, and barely room for our elbows, I urged Sloane to sit and sip and spill her secret.

"I killed a man before," she started.

"Hush up," just kind of popped out of my mouth. "Oh, you're serious?"

"Yes. I was a teenager, visiting my family in Nigeria. We

206

were in Lagos when my great-uncle, who was a prominent journalist exposing the government corruption, received a parcel bomb that blew up and killed him, along with injuring the messenger. The messenger who brought it confessed the details of who hired him, then was found dead the next day."

It sounded like something from a Jack Ryan novel. "Lord have mercy, that's awful!"

"My grandfather could not let it go and sought justice for his dead brother." Sloane paused and hardened, as if reliving the terrible event all over again. "As a result of my grandfather's inquiries, one day another parcel arrived, this one addressed to me. When I saw the terror-stricken expression on the messenger's face as he dropped the package and fled, I ran after him, grabbed him, and used him as a human shield just as the bomb exploded. I killed him, Ginger."

We were both motionless for a long time as her past pulled me in. I didn't feel the need to speak. What could I possibly say?

"The worst part wasn't his mutilated body in my arms. Or his blood and guts on my skin. The unsettling thing is that I would do it again, and sometimes that scares me, Ginger."

"But he knew what he was doing when he delivered the package and ran. It was self-defense what you did."

Sloane's gaze dropped to her mug of tea. "Maybe," she spoke so softly I barely heard her.

I couldn't begin to imagine her experience or her trauma, but I now understood a depth to my friend that made me appreciate her even more. She chose to gift me with her vulnerability, and I would never take it for granted.

Sloane was right. I *did* see her differently. But not the way she imagined. Not as a ruthless killer or a psychologically damaged victim. I saw her strength, and now I understood how she could be so composed in the face of danger. She had endured the worst of it and did what she needed to survive. She had bravely saved herself, and I envied that ability. I continued to shield Rick from the blowback of his mistakes, at the cost of my own life, and almost at the cost of Sloane and Tara's. For once I wanted to let Rick be his own shield.

"Anyway," as if a mask dropped, Sloane regained her cool composure and got back to the business at hand, "I need you to call the police and interpret for me everything that happened during my kidnapping. Plus I have an address where they can find my abductor. If he's still at his house, that is."

"Before I call the cops, tell me what happened from the beginning," I insisted. I wanted to be prepared for anything that might come out.

"You remember when I texted you to come over about the package with the news clipping that I found?"

I nodded.

"Well, shortly after that, my doorbell blinked. When I went to answer it, someone smashed me over the head and knocked me out. Later on the crooked-nosed man mentioned that he had searched my house while I was unconscious, but what he was looking for wasn't there. Then he put a sack over my head, bound and drugged me… and…"

She paused, wiping at the tears streaming down her face. Yes, Sloane usually seemed impenetrable, but even superheroes had breakdowns once in a while. I let her cry as long as she needed to, offering her tissues until the tears soaked her skin, her back grew rigid, and she continued on.

"While I was unconscious he brought me into his house and

tied me up in his basement. Eventually I managed to stab him and escape, but he was still alive when I got away. I don't know if he survived or not. I had to have hit a major artery, I would think."

Sloane described her high-speed getaway, and how she had barely managed to make it out of the house. No, not house, but mansion. So our stalker-shooter-abductor was rich. That at least narrowed it down to the top one percent.

"I can't believe I let this happen…" Sloane bemoaned. "I wasn't careful enough, Ginger. Especially after getting that package. What more of a warning could he have given me?"

Sloane still bore the youth of reckless assurance. The young always assumed they'd be okay, impervious to the bad things in the world. Unaware that destruction hid in the most ordinary places, tucked within the folds of good things like independence and friendship and romance. The most incredible blessings could be the most painful curses when touched by evil.

"Don't blame yourself, Sloane. You couldn't have done anything different. And by the way, you're a real live action hero!" I exclaimed.

"There's more," she signed.

"More?" How much more could fit into a forty-eight-hour kidnapping?

Sloane grew solemn and watched me uneasily. "I need you to tell me the truth about something. Something my kidnapper told me."

I waited for whatever new level of hell she was about to unleash.

"Do you know anything about a gem?"

I was more confused than a termite in a wooden yo-yo.

What did the gem have to do with Sloane? I could feel the knot unravelling, but I still couldn't find the ends and how it all strung together.

"The gem…" I muttered, wiggling my fingers in the sign for *wait*.

I searched the collection of photos scattered across the breakfast table. When I found the one of Bennie wearing the gaudy thing on a necklace, I passed the picture to her. "Are you talking about this gem?"

Sloane jumped up, hastily signing yes. "Yes, that's it! Please tell me you have it?"

"I'm sorry, but I don't know where it is. Apparently more than one person wants the dangum thing. So much that they would dig up a grave, make us targets in their personal shooting range, and kidnap at least two people to get their hands on it. What the h-e-double hockey sticks makes this ugly thing worth so much money?"

As Sloane set the picture back down, my attention diverted to today's newspaper that I hadn't read yet. I had wondered if the details of the murder at Luna's Restaurant would be covered, and sure enough, the headline screamed about it in black and white:

POLICE SEARCH FOR "GILL"-TY PARTY IN LUNA'S SEAFOOD RESTAURANT SLAYING

I pointed to the headline. "I saw this happen early this morning."

I opened up the paper fully, mumbling under my breath as I read the news story aloud. "I knew it! I'm cursed."

"What?" Sloane signed, unable to read my lips behind the spread.

I lowered the paper to the table for her to read, and tried to formulate some kind of logic for this phenomenon. "I think I'm cursed. There's no other explanation for why so much bad crap follows me everywhere I go. I was at Luna's early this morning when I saw a body getting rolled out, and Detective Hughes was investigating it. I worried the body might have been a bartender I had met there, but instead it was his co-worker. She seemed so nice, too. Such a shame."

Sloane turned her attention to the newspaper and skimmed the article. A woman by the name of Ekaterina Drago, a new hire bartender at Luna's, had been found dead in the empty restaurant.

According to the restaurant's owner, Ms. Drago had met with an unidentified man the night before and was seen having drinks with him at the bar. She was scheduled to close the restaurant that night.

Around three o'clock in the morning the owner got a call from someone claiming to be her boyfriend, requesting the door access code to retrieve her purse that Ekaterina had accidentally left after her shift the night before. When the owner arrived later that morning to start food prep for the day, they found Ekaterina dead.

An unregistered gun was found on Ekaterina's body, and she had a criminal record for theft. After a search of her cell phone records showed ties to Bratva, police suspected foul play. Ingested poisoning, the initial medical examination stated. But the perpetrator was still at large, and the BBPD was asking any witnesses to come forward who might have seen something.

"She had ties to the Russian mafia?" Sloane's eyebrows arched with concern. "Do you think she's our shooter?"

I hadn't considered that sweet little Kat, who let her co-workers flirt with patrons instead of tending bar, could be our flaxen assassin. But all the facts lined up.

"Now that I think about it, she was bartending at Luna's the night Rick disappeared," I confirmed. "Plus I saw a red sports car outside the restaurant after she was killed. Who do you think hired her?"

"Do you know anyone with ties to the Russia mob? Maybe Ewan Valance?"

Considering how chauvinistic he was, it seemed unlikely that he would associate with a *woman*, let alone a Russian woman. That kind of connection coming out would easily cost him his well-protected public image, along with an election.

"It doesn't sound like him." Something Sloane had said earlier triggered a thought. "Did you say the man who abducted you had a crooked nose?"

"Yes, why?"

Then it dawned on me. A memory from a long time ago that had faded into the many pages of my mental scrapbook over the years. It came back now crisp and clear. The details clicked together, little moments piled up, one on top of the other, like a slideshow projected in the front of my mind. The realization felt so heavy I collapsed back into my chair.

"Jiminy cricket, I think I know who it is!"

Chapter 35

"Was the man who kidnapped you really ugly, with demon-black eyes, and a hooked nose and pointy teeth?" was my first question for Sloane.

Pursing her lips, she knew not to take my description seriously, but she did light up at bit with recognition.

"No, he wasn't a Marvel comics villain, Ginger." She grinned slightly, which meant I had achieved my objective. "But he did have a bent nose and a contorted smile."

"And slicked-back hair like he'd doused it with oil?" I added.

"Yes! That's him. Do you know him?"

She confirmed exactly who I had suspected it to be.

"Corbin Roth. It *has* to be him. Did he mention if Rick was… still alive?"

I was all set to Google Roth's home address and rescue Rick myself. And of course go to the police with Sloane's story, like I had promised.

Until Sloane stopped me.

"Wait, Ginger, you're getting ahead of yourself. Roth is not the one who kidnapped Rick."

How was it *not* Roth? Two different archvillains in the same small town? What were the odds? Slim, if I were to venture a guess. But then again, in Bloodson Bay we defied all odds.

"Are you sure? Did he actually tell you he didn't have Rick? Because he might have been lying."

"No, he wasn't lying. He's looking for Rick too. He claims Rick double-crossed him over that gem. Rick was supposed to steal it for Corbin, but he ended up taking it for himself."

Click went a puzzle piece into place. So that was the origin where the whole gem mystery started, and it explained how Rick got sucked into this deadly game of hide-and-seek. I should have known Corbin Roth was behind it. But another piece of the puzzle was still missing. I didn't have the whole story. What did Sloane have to do with Rick and the gem?

"It still doesn't explain why Roth went after *you,* Sloane. Did he think you got hold of the gem or knew something about it?"

"You could say that…"

Sloane sucked in a shaky breath, exhaling with an audible sigh. "I found out something that could end our friendship, Ginger."

"Wha—I don't understand. What could possibly come between us?" It sounded an awful lot like Sloane was about to break up with me.

"It involves Rick and the gem," she began. "And something unforgiveable that *your husband* did to *my father.*"

Then she told me a heartbreakingly beautiful but terrible story that would disrupt my entire world and cast my future in gray.

Long ago, Sloane's father worked for Doctors Without Borders. During his travels he saved many lives, but there was one life in particular that changed him.

214

Sloane's mother, Alika.

After curing her from malaria that had spread throughout her tribe, his fondness for her blossomed into love. He sought her father's blessing to take her hand in marriage but was denied. Three times.

He couldn't provide for Alika, they told him. Their daughter was already betrothed to another, they said. And so the Apara family insisted he leave, forget Alika, and move on. So he did. Sort of.

He left, but he never moved on.

Months passed, and he found himself working in Australia among the Aborigines. After saving the life of a tribesman's wife, he had been given the gem as a thank-you. That gem would prove his worth to Alika's family, so he returned to Nigeria with the gem in hand.

His plan worked. Alika's father blessed the marriage, with two caveats. She must keep her tribal name, and he must always provide for her. He easily agreed to both.

That gem was the first gift he gave to Alika. With it they planned to finance their new life in America. But as with all best-laid plans, this one didn't just go awry. It ended in murder.

Eventually Corbin Roth caught wind of the gem's worth when Alika's father went to the jeweler to get it assessed. A value of $150,000 in 1979, the jeweler had discovered, which translated the modern worth to a ballpark of $800,000.

That was the beginning of the end as Roth hired someone to steal it from her unsuspecting father. But a simple theft took a deadly turn as the thief put her dad in a coma for nearly a year, until he died of complications. He was *murdered* in cold blood. Which was why the newspaper clipping was left at Sloane's house:

Your husband was killed. You are next.

This message wasn't about Rick, or Chris. It was meant for Alika Apara, whose husband was killed and whose family was now a target not just of Roth, but of some other cloak-and-dagger newspaper-delivering stalker who also knew about the gem and Sloane's connection to it.

But Sloane had left out the most important part of the story. I dreaded how this would end. I didn't want to know. I sensed this knowledge would change everything. But Sloane was my friend, and friends sometimes had to make the hard choices, sacrifices in the name of friendship.

"Who was the man Roth hired to steal the gem, Sloane? The thief who killed your father?"

She shook her head, unwilling to tell me.

"Sloane," I rested my hand on her arm, "you have to tell me."

The wheels were already turning. Alika's husband had been murdered over a gem, and Rick had never told me how he had gotten his hands on it. I didn't need super-sleuthing skills to figure this out. A terribly easy game of connect-the-dots.

"It was Rick, wasn't it?"

Sloane didn't need to confirm what I suspected. While Sloane wept and I wept, we both mourned a loss that day. Hers was the death of the mystery behind her father's killer. But mine was the loss of the marriage I had hoped to save.

I now understood why Sloane had said this revelation would end our friendship. I knew what she wanted from me.

"Are you willing to turn Rick in for what he did to my father?" she asked.

Rick would never forgive me if I did, and Sloane would never forgive me if I didn't. Everything in me wanted to tell her yes, that I would make sure Rick got the punishment he deserved. But by punishing him, I would be punishing myself, too. Goodbye to my happy ending that I had been fighting for and hoping for, the whole reason I kept searching for him.

"I don't know what to say, Sloane…"

"Just think about it, Ginger. The fact that Rick put you in the middle of this mess should tell you everything you need to know about the man you're so quick to give up everything for—including your friend."

Sloane left me in my kitchen with a lot to think about and a lot of soul-searching. Not that I could end any of this now. I was already in too deep to quit. The only way out was through—through finding Rick.

As I considered what the news clippings had been telling me, I had assumed they were a threat:

Rick is missing.
If you go to police Rick will die.
Fourteen.
Your husband was killed. You are next.

The first one started the search. The second protected his life. The third led me to Rick. And the fourth revealed the connection to Sloane's family history.

WHAT SHE DOESN'T KNOW

All this time I had it wrong. The messages had never been a threat. They had been a warning.

Chapter 36

Rick had done a lot of despicable things in his life, but I had always found the heart to forgive him, because every bad choice had been his way of trying to take care of me:

He worked for Corbin Roth so he could buy me my dream horse.

He helped bury Judge Ewan Valance's crimes so he could buy me my dream house.

The problem was that Rick had missed out on my actual dream—to build a family together. I could forgive much, until he crossed a line I could never forgive. He killed an innocent man—my friend's father—to feed his greed. Rick didn't deserve to be rescued from whoever had taken him, and I was no longer doing it for Rick or for me, but for Sloane.

Because the moment I saved Rick, I would finally give Sloane and her mother justice by turning him in. I would get over the man who continuously broke my heart when he broke his promises, and I knew just how to jumpstart that rebound process.

After Ekaterina's dead body had been found in Luna's Restaurant, I was surprised to see the restaurant was open today. It was late, near closing, when I pulled into the parking lot where only a handful of vehicles remained. I hoped one of them was

Gunther's.

A rumble of thunder threatened rain as I hustled through the light drizzle. Inside the blessedly warm, dry, empty lobby, Gunther's smile greeted me the instant our eyes met. He was wiping the bar counter down with a rag when I approached, both nervous and excited. I planned to ask him out on a date, something I had never done before but which Tara assured me *modern* women were doing these days. I hadn't been modern since the 1970s, but I'd give it a try.

Tonight only.

For one man only.

"Hey there, beautiful," Gunther gushed as I propped my elbows on the bar. "What can I get you tonight? Another grasshopper?"

I pretended to think it over. "I'm more in the mood for all-you-can-eat waffles at Debbie's Diner."

Gunther pretended to look outside. "It's a little late for breakfast, don't you think? Unless you're suggesting hanging out until morning." He grinned slyly and leaned over the counter.

Clearly he wasn't going to make this easy for me. "Haven't you ever heard of breakfast for dinner—*brinner*?"

He chuckled. "I actually haven't. I guess I've been sheltered."

"Well?"

"Well what?"

"Do. You. Want. To. Join. Me. For. Brinner?" He was making me spell it out for him, and I was enjoying it immensely.

"Are you asking me out on a date, Ginger Boyle?" And another butter-melting smile I had grown so fond of so quickly.

"Only if you like waffles. If you don't, then the offer is off the table. I can't abide a date with an anti-brinner waffle-hater."

He laughed and tossed the rag in a bin behind him, then grabbed a jacket and newspaper that had been sitting on a table. Pressing his palm to the bar counter, he pushed his lanky body up and swung his legs over in an impressively deft bar exit. Hitting a perfect landing, he propped one black boot on the bottom rung of the stool and leaned toward me, making my head swoon. He had become Tom Cruise in *Cocktail*.

"I happen to adore waffles, *and* breakfast for dinner, but only if I'm paying. Will you let me take you out to brinner tonight?"

"It sounds like the tables have turned. I suppose I'll tolerate you stealing my thunder. But just so you know, I had worked hard mustering the courage to ask you out, then you just turn it around on me?" I teased.

"Is that a yes?"

"How could I say no?"

I led the way out of the restaurant into what had escalated from a drizzle to a light shower. When you lived in a coastal farming community during hurricane season, you paid attention to the fine differences in the weather.

"I heard about your friend who was killed this morning." I hoped it wasn't tacky of me to bring it up. I wasn't exactly known for my tact.

"Who—Kat? Oh, she wasn't a friend. Just a co-worker," he corrected me. "The police are still investigating. I hope they find whoever did it."

"Any thoughts on who?"

"Well, you may have read the news about her Russian mafia

connection. So there's no telling who she might have associated with, or who would want her dead."

"Yeah, I figured as much. I still feel bad for her, though. I'm sure she didn't dream of being a hit woman as a little girl." Even the worst criminals had been innocent little babies at one point.

We walked to his car side by side, his free hand bumping against my thigh in welcome little shocks of touch. I glanced down, noticing the newspaper he carried.

"I thought I was the only one left on this planet who read physical newspapers."

"No, there's actually a club for us. You should join. It's mostly old-fashioned geezers like me, so you'd be a refreshing youthful addition."

Oh, he was good!

We stopped at Gunther's car, a 1975 Porsche Turbo. Better known as the Widowmaker. Once upon a time Rick had a friend who owned one, and he talked the car up like it could fly or teleport. To me cars were just slabs of metal that got you from point A to point B. Unless it was a monster truck—one of those could practically fly!

"Nice ride." I pretended to ooh and ahh because I knew men liked their egos stroked, and I wanted to make sure I did this whole dating thing right this time.

"I bought her brand new in '75. Can you believe that she still looks this good?"

"I always felt that age brings out more beauty each year." I flipped my hair back with my hand awkwardly, trying to play cool but failing miserably. "You never wanted to upgrade to something newer?"

"And deal with all microchips and computerized parts

always breaking? No thanks. I can fix this baby up with my own bare hands, and she still runs like a dream." He turned his gaze on me. "Plus, I don't believe in trading in an older, beautiful classic for a new, cookie-cutter younger model. I tend to be pretty committed to the things I love."

The fine hairs on my neck sprouted up. Were we still talking about the car? Or was he confessing that he *loved* me?

I glanced inside the car through the rain-dappled glass, noticing how clean it was. With just a purse and some gum in the center console, it was OCD clean compared to my hoard on wheels that held everything from an extra pair of underwear (you never knew when you'd need 'em) to an ice scraper that proved itself obsolete in our mild North Carolina winters. The entire town shut down if even a dusting of snow was predicted.

Seeing the purse, I realized I had never officially confirmed that Gunther was single. How stupid was I to assume he was available? This was why I preferred to stay old-fashioned and didn't ask men out on dates.

"Before we go on our brinner date," my nerves were spazzing like a teen before prom, "are you… available?"

"Available as in single? Yes, Ginger, I'm not a cheater, if that's what you're worried about."

I hesitated to get into his Porsche, uncertain that it was wise to ride with him. So he wasn't a cheater, but that didn't mean he wasn't a serial killer. With a smile like that, he was probably slaying women left and right. And if I did end up kissing Gunther, would I be a cheater, since technically I was still married to Rick?

Why was dating so darn complicated?

"We should probably drive separately," I suggested,

shivering through my soaked shirt at the unusually cool night for September.

"That's fine. I can follow you," he agreed. "Here, take my jacket. That way I can be sure you won't try to ditch me. Otherwise you'll be stealing my jacket and you don't strike me as a thief."

How could I ever mistake such a gentleman for a serial killer?

Gunther slipped his black leather jacket over my damp shoulders, and while the cold, stiff leather did nothing to warm me, Gunther's touch nearly set me on fire. The giddy schoolgirl in me resurfaced as I snagged a lock of red hair and dreamily twirled it around my finger.

"I'll meet you at Debbie's!" I called over my shoulder.

I headed to my car, grinning like a possum eating a sweet potato, when I noticed the tightness of the jacket. It actually fit me. Considering Gunther was much larger than me, how did he even wear this? I gave the jacket a more thorough examination, noticing blonde hairs stuck to the lapel.

Blonde, like Kat's hair. In quick succession my brain rattled off clue by clue: The woman's purse in Gunther's car—was that the one Kat had accidentally left at Luna's? Then there was the newspaper that only old-fashioned geezers carried. Geezers that might still have newspapers from the 1970s?

"What's wrong, Ginger?" He was hanging halfway out of his vehicle when his voice scraped the smile off my lips.

I didn't want to believe that Gunther was working with Kat, the woman who shot at us. Or that he might have been the one who killed her. Or that he was the one who abducted Rick. But one little obscure detail tied everything together… and I knew right then and there that Gunther had been behind it all.

My name.

He knew my maiden name, Ginger Boyle, which I had never told him and hadn't gone by in fifty years.

I shivered, but not from the cold. Or the rain that was starting to sprinkle. I was wearing murder evidence—Kat's jacket. And her killer was standing barely ten feet away.

We were completely alone in the parking lot, with only a single streetlight that barely reached the shadows where we were parked. The mist coming off the bay surrounded the light in a glistening haze.

I aimed my key fob at my door, but with my slippery hands trembling, I dropped them and watched them slide under the car.

"Sugar, honey, iced tea!" I screamed in frustration.

I knelt down, searching for my keys, finding the glistening metal just out of reach behind the front tire. I needed to get into the safety of my car before Gunther realized I had figured him out. I knew who he was, who he worked for, and what he had done.

When my finger hooked around the key ring and I stood up, it was already too late. I bumped into Gunther's chest and let out a squeak. Grabbing my wrists, his fingers bit into my skin, pinning my arms against the car. An intensity tightened his jaw as he glared down at me.

I yelped as he pressed harder against me, rendering me immobile. He was too big and too strong for me to escape.

"Why are you making me do this to you, Ginger? Why won't you just give me what I want?"

I tried to reach inside myself and pull out the right words that would make him free me. If I knew what he wanted to hear,

I would mold them just right. But I didn't know what Gunther wanted, or what he was willing to do to get it.

Chapter 37

BLOODSON BAY BULLETIN
November 8, 1973

SHOULD A GENTLEMAN OFFER A TIPARILLO TO A VIOLINIST?

After a tough evening with the Beethoven crowd, she loves to relax and listen to her folk-rock records. Preferably on your stereo. This violinist is open-minded. So tonight you offer her a Tiparillo cigarette, the slim cigar with a white tip. Elegant. Well, should you offer? After all, if she likes your offer, she might start to play. With you. No strings attached.

"I will definitely miss our little games, Ginger." Gunther released his hold on my wrist, angling for my hand. He squeezed until my keys popped out of my fist, and I noticed a folded paper in his other hand.

"You call this a game? Games are Monopoly or Life. Not murder and death." I tugged my hand free of his grip, lunged for my keys and missed as he held them out of my reach. "Are you going to kill me or let me go?"

"You're just going to give up that quickly? Don't tell me you want to quit before you even find Rick. The Ginger I know would fight until the end."

"First of all," I raised a finger and wagged it at him, "you don't know me. And secondly, is there any point to fighting anymore? Isn't Rick dead?"

He pressed closer, his body trapping mine. I glanced around at the empty street. The last car had left the Luna's parking lot. The rain had driven everyone inside. There was no one to call out to for help.

"Wouldn't it be a relief if he *was* dead, Ginger?"

What kind of question was that? Or was this all part of the *games* he was so intent on playing? I refused to be the mouse to his cat. If I was going to die, at least today I was wearing cute underwear and I could go in dignity.

"Please, just kill me and get it over with, because I'm tired of the wait."

His clean-shaven jaw pulsed, and his grip loosened. I realized then how very different he was from Rick in his clean-cut clothes and thoughtful demeanor, yet he hid the exact same darkness inside. Shuffling back half a step, he reached for his pocket, where I imagined his weapon of choice to be. Then he pulled out a—

I nearly collapsed in relief as I saw a stick of gum. He unwrapped it and dropped it on his tongue, tucking the wrapper back into his pocket. He may have been a killer, but at least he didn't litter.

"Kill you?" He popped a bubble, then continued chewing.

"I'm trying to help you, Ginger."

"Help me? By scaring me to death? Or by shooting at me and my friends, kidnapping Sloane, and putting a bomb on Chris's plane?"

He laughed, a strange sound. Almost psychotic.

"I had nothing to do with Ekaterina shooting at you. That was Corbin Roth who put a hit on you. I was trying to protect you from him. Roth doesn't know that I… defected, if you want to call it that. But I'm not working for Roth anymore. I'm working for myself."

"You're after the gem too?"

"Heck no. I want nothing to do with it. I'm just trying to keep myself out of prison and keep you safe."

"Prove it," I dared him.

"Why do you think I called in that *fake* bomb threat? That was me—trying to keep Chris from coming home and putting himself into Corbin Roth's line of fire! Roth wasn't going to stop at anything to get what he wanted, even if it meant going after everyone Rick—and you—cared about. Including Chris, Tara, Sloane… and most importantly, you."

Although I was still terrified of him, somehow I believed that he wasn't here to hurt me. The messages—they had been intended to warn me in order to protect me. But there was still something missing…

"If you were trying to help me, then tell me where you stashed Rick."

"I can't do that."

"Why not?"

"Because as long as he's tucked away, you'll be safe."

This was getting exasperating. "Look, I can't make you tell

me anything, but I can protect myself, Gunther… if that's your real name."

He exhaled an air of disappointment.

"Of course it's Gunther. Gunther Jones. I can't believe you don't remember me."

"Should I?"

"I would think so, but I had a feeling you hadn't. So I saved this to refresh your memory."

He handed me back my keys, along with the paper he had been holding, a wrinkled little square. It was one last news clipping, similar to all the others with an underlined message meant only for me. I mentally pieced together all the letters, reading it out loud:

T urn over gem to free ric

"It seems everything revolves around that darn gem! If I give it to you, you'll free Rick, huh? How do I know he's still alive?"

"Because I never had any intention of killing him, Ginger. I'm not a killer."

"Bologna. You killed your co-worker, Kat."

He threw his hands up, shaking his head. "No way, Ginger. First of all, Kat and I initially were working together to try to save you. But then Corbin Roth must have gotten to her and offered her a bigger payday that I could give her. I only realized it when she double-crossed me and went after you. But I didn't kill her. That wasn't me."

"Sure it wasn't. Then why do you have her purse?"

"I saw her car here the night she died. I wanted to talk to her privately, hoping to convince her not to go after Rick anymore. But when I tried the doors, they were locked and she wasn't answering. So I called the owners, claiming to be her boyfriend and making some excuse about her leaving her purse inside. They gave me the access code, but when I found her inside, she was already dead. I took her purse and coat in case there was any evidence that connected her to me. I forgot to grab her gun, though."

"I don't believe you. You're a kidnapper, a liar, and a killer, Gunther. And you have a weird obsession with newspapers, by the way. Why do you have so many from the 1970s, anyway?"

He shrugged. "Evidence. In case I ever needed to use them against Roth. Messages between Roth and his men were sent through ads back then. As for why I used them to communicate with you, I was trying to be original. And untraceable. I'm not a big fan of modern technology, if you couldn't tell."

Maybe he wasn't as strange as I thought, but still… pretty darn crazy.

"You're a criminal, Gunther. Plain and simple. And criminals can't be trusted."

"You really think that of me? Is it because of my cousin? Because I'm nothing like him."

"Your cousin? Are you talking about Corbin Roth?"

"Ha! No, I *wish* my cousin was Roth! My cousin makes Roth look like Mother Teresa. Try again. Here's a hint: He's evil incarnate. You don't remember meeting him?" He was so intense I could feel his energy, so close his body heat warmed me. "Look at the date on the article, Ginger. I really wanted you to remember me on your own, but I guess you might need a little nudge."

The sepia paper was stained with dark dots as the rain chewed away at its integrity.

"Oh, come on! It was fifty years ago, Gunther. You can't blame an old lady for forgetting some random date in November of 1973."

"I guess I'm the only one who never forgot it, then. That's embarrassing."

I wracked my brain, pulling up the date. A lot had happened in 1973. But November 8? It felt strongly familiar.

In fact, this whole moment felt familiar, like déjà vu. Standing in the rain, bodies so close I felt weak. His leather jacket slung over my shoulders. Only instead of Gunther it was Rick.

That was it. That was all the nudge I needed in order to remember.

Chapter 38

November 8, 1973

I hated when Rick and I fought. But I hated it even more when we should have been fighting but weren't.

Silent treatment was a bummer to the max.

"You ready to talk to me?" Rick's voice was barely audible over the crashing waves tonight.

I stared at the ocean with my house aglow behind me. I could always tell when the weather was turning based on how the sea reacted to it. When she was calm, the weather followed her easy stride. But when she was ornery, we never knew what kind of storm to expect.

Leaving a living room full of strangers groovin' to the Rolling Stones in *my* house, Rick found me on the beach where I had managed to escape talks of Peoples Temple and San Francisco that I wanted no part of.

Apparently Rick's new friend Jim Jones, who he only just met a few weeks ago, had been scouting the East Coast looking for ripe towns to plant his next church in. Bloodson Bay proved not to be "Black enough," whatever that meant. A white man actively seeking Black female followers sounded creepy enough to wave a big red flag. Luckily Jim decided to head back to California, then on to Guyana, hoping to convince Rick to go with him as one of his growing followers.

I had no right to tell Rick not to go. It wasn't like we were married or anything. And yet the fact that Rick was considering leaving me told me where his heart truly was. Not with me, the girl he had professed his undying love to only two months earlier.

"If you want to go, I won't stop you," I warned. "But I'll tell you one thing. That Jim Jones is not to be trusted, Rick. He makes crazy claims, and I have a bad feeling that if you go with him to Guyana, you'll never come back."

Rick was quiet for a long time, just him and me standing in the rain. Then he removed his beloved red leather jacket, placed it on my shoulders, and fell to one knee.

"Then marry me, Gingersnap. Give me a reason not to go."

He had asked me several times before, but my parents had been against it. Against us.

Too young. Too wild. Too dumb. There were a million reasons to say no, but only one reason to say yes. I loved him. To me, that sole reason was enough.

It didn't take a single thought for the *yes* to come out, because I had loved Rick from the moment I met him. I loved how he loved me. That he would rather follow a crazy preacher man across the ocean to a remote commune than live here and not be able to be fully with me.

"Yes, Rick, of course I'll marry you!"

He jumped up, grabbing me in his arms and swinging me around while the rain showered us with its blessing.

"This girl is going to be my wife!" Rick yelled to the sky, which boomed back at him. "We've got to celebrate!"

Grabbing my hand, he ran toward the house, pulling me

along beside him in an endorphin-fueled happy haze. Dark agitated clouds framed the bright dwelling, as if they had decided to congregate there as a warning. When we ran under the porch awning, giggling and shivering, Rick headed into the kitchen to proclaim the good news while I stayed behind to shake the rain off my clothes.

A man came out, his face and ponytail of curls an obscure silhouette against the kitchen window. Walking up to me, he stood so close that his tall, slender form felt familiar but unknown. He had kept me company for hours while Jim preached at Rick about the benefits of Communism.

Although we had never exchanged names, we discussed everything from the Watergate Scandal to Pink Floyd to *The Exorcist*. He captivated me with his thoughts, and entertained me with his humor. If I had been single… well… I banished that thought because I wasn't. In fact, it was quite the opposite, because I was officially engaged!

"I guess congratulations are in order then?" he asked shyly, as if searching for confirmation.

It was clear this was no congratulatory speech.

"Uh, yeah, thanks. Word on the street is that you're Jim Jones's cousin?" I didn't need to ask. This man, and our intense conversation, was memorable.

He nodded. "Unfortunately."

"Why unfortunately?"

"Because my cousin is a narcissistic psycho. Anyway, enough about my dysfunctional family. Let's talk about yours." He chuckled, lightening the mood.

"No psychos in my family tree. That I know of. Unless maybe I'm the first…" I made a shrill imitation of the infamous shower-scene song from *Psycho*, holding my hand in a fist while miming a blade stabbing downward.

He laughed, then I laughed, and it felt so good to be in his presence. Too good.

"Anyway, are you returning to California with Jim?"

"Hell no." He looked around us, eyes trailing the beach. "I think I might stick around here. Head up and down the East Coast. Unless…"

"Unless what?" I fished. I couldn't explain why my heart started thrumming so wildly.

"Unless Bloodson Bay has something—or someone—that might be worth staying here for."

I laughed, partly because it was an unbelievably silly notion to consider giving up Rick for a man whose name I didn't even know. The other part of me didn't feel it was all that unbelievable.

"I don't think I ever got your name," I said.

"Gunther Jones. And yours?"

"Ginger Boyle."

The kitchen door swung open, while Rick hung out the door beckoning me with a drunken cat call.

"Your knight in shining armor awaits," Gunther said after Rick disappeared back inside. "You know you could do so much better, don't you?"

I pulled open the kitchen door, pausing in the glow. "What makes you think you're so much better?"

Chapter 39

Gunther Jones still thought he was nothing like the men he had associated with, but I saw their shadows within him.

"Climb in," I ordered, unlocking the car door and sliding into the driver's seat. After Gunther settled into the passenger seat beside me, I inhaled a calming breath. "I never meant to lead you on. You knew I was engaged, though. You even congratulated me."

"It was stupid of me to fall for you. I get that. I guess I had just hoped you wouldn't forget me so easily. I never forgot you. Even after all these years."

Coulda, shoulda, woulda. I *couldn't* go back in time, and I *shouldn't* assume anything would have been better with Gunther Jones instead of Rick Mallowan. I *wouldn't* put myself through this again.

After all, Gunther had abducted Rick and Rick had killed Sloane's father—were they really that different from one another?

"Well, we all make our choices. Some good, some bad. Then we have to live with them. But there's one choice you have right now, Gunther. The one that really matters."

"What choice is that?" He leaned toward me expectantly, as if I was about to offer myself, my holy kiss.

I angled back. "The choice to save Rick, you dumbass! To right your wrongs. Unless... you didn't already kill him, did you?"

"I already told you no, of course not! I've always considered Rick a friend."

"Is that normal to go around beating up and abducting your friends?"

Finally I got Gunther to cave. "Okay, okay. So I'm a crappy friend. And I only beat him up because he was resisting. But he's secure in a storage unit. I even gave you a clue for exactly where to find him. I guess you didn't figure it out."

"Of course I figured it out and went to the storage unit. Number fourteen. It wasn't that hard to decipher, by the way. You're talking to one of Tara's Angels, the super-sleuths of Bloodson Bay." I chuckled, but based on Gunther's perplexed expression, he hadn't heard of us. Not that Tara's Angels had gone public. Yet. Maybe after solving this caper we would.

"Tara's Angels?" Gunther asked.

"You know, three crime-fighting hot chicks. Kind of like *Charlie's Angels*, but with Tara as our leader instead. Though I'm starting to think I'm the brains of the group. We may need to rebrand."

Gunther rolled his hand, urging me to move my story along. "You went to the storage unit and...?"

"Oh yeah, and Rick wasn't there."

"What do you mean he wasn't there?" Gunther shouted too loud for such a small space.

"Just what I said. The chair was empty, there was blood on the floor, his bindings were off. And no Rick."

I rooted in my purse, feeling around. When I felt the thin

strands of plastic, I pulled out the zip ties that I had picked up off the floor, holding them out to show Gunther how they had been cut.

Gunther groaned. "Someone must have gotten to him…"

"What do you mean? You *lost* your captive?"

"Well…" he stammered. "I didn't lose him. Someone else must have found him."

"Who, Gunther? Who would have stumbled on an abandoned storage unit last used in the 1970s and stolen my missing husband? Because I already know it's not Corbin Roth, since he's looking for him too."

"What about Ewa—" Gunther began, but I was already moving on.

"And it's not one of the Valances, since Leonard is in jail and his dad wouldn't risk getting involved with Rick."

Gunther ticked each name off on his fingers, then mumbled, "The only other person who knew where I stashed him was Kat."

"And Kat is now dead. So who else is left, Gunther?"

His face paled as shock settled in. "I don't know, Ginger. I don't know."

"I still don't understand why you abducted him. What was the point—if not to get your grubby hands on the gem?"

Gunther scoffed. "I could care less about that cursed jewel. Like I said, I did it to protect you before Rick did something stupid that would end up killing you."

"What do you mean? How was making me a target protecting me?" I couldn't wait to hear the logic behind this as Gunther took me back to 1979…

Chapter 40

December 9, 1979

"I did something bad, G." Rick's face was covered in sweat and his body shivered like he had the flu.

Gunther led him through Roth's Auto Repair, a mechanic shop by day and chop shop by night. Rick and Gunther had been in the middle of tearing apart a stolen 1978 Cadillac that Roth intended to sell. All under the table, and all illegal.

"It can't be that bad, Rick." But Gunther didn't know the half of it.

Rick paced around the Caddie, running his hands through his hair. "Oh, it's bad, man. Worse than bad. A few days ago I stabbed a man and put him in a coma over a jewel."

Okay, so it was worse than Gunther could have imagined. Like, *in jail for life* kind of worse.

"I need to turn myself in," Rick added after a beat. "I can't live with the guilt. Every time I look at Ginger I feel it all over again. The shame of what I did and what I'm hiding from her."

Stopping Rick mid-pace, Gunther grabbed Rick's shoulders, shaking some sense into him.

"If you turn yourself in, you're going to end up dead, Rick. Roth won't let you confess and get away with it."

Rick's face faded to a whole new shade of pale.

"What if I don't mention Roth?" Rick argued. "I'll say I did it on my own. Maybe the guy will survive and I'll just get charged with armed robbery, but no homicide."

Gunther stepped back and interlocked his fingers behind his neck as he thought it over.

"Aggravated robbery will cost you twenty or more years, Rick. Doesn't matter if he survives or not. If he does die, then it's life. But twenty years, man?" He rubbed his chin. "That's most of your life anyway!"

Rick threw his hands up in defeat. "I'm already not living as it is. I can't keep doing this to Ginger… hiding things from my wife, man."

"If you tell, you'll be throwing us *all* under the bus, Rick. It doesn't just affect you. We'll all go to jail. And best-case scenario, it's just jail. You know Roth has no qualms about silencing rats—or their family members—permanently. You know how he likes to make an example of people!"

"You don't think he'd actually… kill Ginger, do you?"

"That's exactly what I think he'd do. He'd kill your wife just to make a point to the rest of us. That's what guys like him do. They murder to force their men to think twice before crossing them. Look at what my own cousin did to more than 900 of his loyal followers! He made them kill themselves in a mass suicide with that poisoned Jim Jones juice, all because people wanted to leave his crazy compound."

Rick strode across the shop, leaning on the half-dismantled brown Cadillac at shoulder height on the car lift. It still needed gutted… which brought to Rick's mind a horrible, bloody image of missing entrails.

"If I bring the cops evidence against Roth, maybe they'll

offer me a deal. If you join me, I bet we can both get a plea. Get Corbin Roth *and* Ewan Valance behind bars in one fell swoop."

Gunther reached over and patted Rick's cheek.

"Dude, you gotta live with your guilt. You talking is a death sentence for your wife. And that jewel that I know you're hiding from Roth, you better get rid of it. Because if he finds out you double-crossed him—and he will, because even I figured it out—you *and* Ginger are as good as dead."

"I already feel as good as dead inside, G. What if that man dies?"

"Do you love Ginger?" Gunther asked pointedly.

"More than anything. So much I'm willing to turn myself in to be the man she always thought I was—a good man who does the right thing."

"If you love her, you'll never speak of the jewel, or the man you stabbed, or any of it ever again. You'll die with the secret of what you did."

Rick dropped his head to the Cadillac's hood, banging his brow against the metal. "How? I can't sleep, even with pills, I have no appetite, I'm a crappy husband who doesn't deserve Ginger… and now you're telling me I can't right my wrongs, or get out of this life of crime, or turn myself in… otherwise I'll sentence my wife to death? What am I supposed to do? How can I go home to Ginger telling a lie this big?"

Gunther lowered his mouth to Rick's ear. "You keep your head down, keep your mouth shut, and hope that one day someone puts a hit on Roth and Valance so we can finally be free."

"And if I don't?" Rick dared, turning to look at his friend, the only one he trusted.

Gunther's eye twitched as it locked on Rick. His Adam's apple bobbed as he swallowed. Rick knew this look, this side of Gunther that made him disturbing, but also exceedingly good at his job. Compartmentalizing his emotions was something Rick had never gotten the hang of, nor did he ever want to after seeing what it did to his friend. Turned him ruthless, animalistic… unpredictable.

"Then I'll be forced to shut you up for your own good."

Rick believed every word.

Chapter 41

I wanted to tell Gunther that I didn't need him to protect me from Corbin Roth or Ewan Valance. As a single working mom, I had been taking care of myself all my life, and nothing was tougher than a broke mom with boys to raise.

I didn't say it, though.

I appreciated his offer so much that a tiny part of me hungered to give him that long-awaited kiss because he *wanted* to protect me. That, and he was as fine as a frog hair split four ways.

I didn't kiss him, either.

Instead I left Gunther in the Luna's Restaurant parking lot, working my brain in a frenzy over where the heck Rick could have gotten himself dragged to now. And who was doing the dragging.

It was almost three o'clock in the morning as I sat in my breakfast nook with every meager clue spread out in front of me on the table. My brain was as alert as a college kid before an exam. I knew in my gut that Rick was alive, just as I knew I would find him. I couldn't explain how, just that my gut was never wrong. Except for the time it told me to eat the weeks-old leftovers in the fridge that later gave me food poisoning.

Dumping the contents of my purse out, I pulled out the zip

ties and examined them. The cut edges in particular. They weren't smooth like I would imagine they should be from someone cutting them with a proper tool, though. They were rough and jagged… almost reminiscent of teeth marks. Like someone had chewed through them.

I knew from years of love-making how bendable Rick could be in the boudoir. On many nights we had reenacted our own little circus acrobatics. Certainly it wouldn't be beyond the realm of possibility for him to contort himself while tied to a chair…

Which meant that someone might not have taken him, but he freed himself.

"Oh, Rick, you rascal! You better hope you're dead," I muttered.

That should have been great news, except for the part that he never bothered to tell me he was okay. Had he gotten free and left without a goodbye? No proof of life so that I wouldn't have to worry and wonder for the rest of my days? He had promised me he would never do that to me again… and from where I was sitting, it looked like another broken promise.

I wasn't sure I even wanted to find him. He deserved to stay on the run, as far away from me as possible so he could never break my heart again.

In a fury I got up from my seat, grabbed the garbage can, and dragged it to the table. Scooping up piles of papers, I tossed them handful by handful in the garbage.

Spread out before me were photographs, memorabilia, the funeral sign-in book, and all of the news clippings. I wanted it all gone! I reached for a box to add to the purge, then stopped short of pitching Bennie's memorial book into the trashcan.

It was open to the page where Ewan Valance's name had been signed, along with Corbin Roth's. At the very bottom, on the last line, there wasn't a name but a message to Bennie beyond the grave:

To my little Pee-wee, we'll ride again soon together in heaven. Daddy loves you.

Rick had been at the funeral. He had never mentioned it to me, but since they had been in contact right before Bennie passed, when Rick sold him the horse, maybe Rick had kept an eye on his son from afar. It was a nice thought to consider, a father looking out for his grown kid until the very end.

Something not-so-nice crowded out that thought, jostling for my head space. If Rick had been at the funeral, and Bennie had been wearing the gem, and the gem disappeared... and now Rick disappeared... like dominos pushing the next over, the facts fell at my fingertips. Rick had taken the gem off of Bennie at the funeral. I hadn't noticed much of anything that day, through the tears and anxiety and frequent trips to the wash room to splash cool water on my face. But it seemed like I knew everything there was to know.

Except for where Rick was now.

A cardboard box sat in the middle of the table collecting Bennie's more valuable belongings, things I could drop off at the children's home donation center. As a boy, Bennie had idolized his absentee father, drilling me for details on what his dad was like, what movies he watched, what foods were his favorite. One time I had mentioned Rick's love for all things John Wayne, so that year for Christmas Bennie asked for a movie poster featuring the Duke. An old framed movie poster of the 1976 *The Shootist* poked out of the cardboard box.

So many keys to the past sat on this table, but none of it pointed me to Rick's whereabouts, or why he would have left me again without a goodbye. I picked up the box, moving it to the floor, and behind it my gaze settled on a vase of pink carnations. The same exact flowers from the table at Luna's the night Rick had gone missing, as fresh and vibrant as ever.

Except I hadn't brought any carnations home.

I definitely left them there. Which meant… only Rick would have dropped off the flowers that represented our first *I love yous*. A sign that he had escaped and was okay. A clue that he would never leave me to wonder again. How had I missed this?

Rick wanted me to find him, but where would he hide if he was on the run from Corbin Roth or the Bratva? I thought about the gem, where he had hidden it.

The best place to hide is in plain sight.

I had quoted him those very words on the beach the day he disappeared.

As a real-estate developer, I imagined that Corbin Roth had a lot of vacant properties where he hid drugs and guns and many other god-awful things he illegally trafficked. One of those locations would be the most likely place Rick would go, since he knew which ones hadn't been used for decades and would most likely avoid Roth's radar. It would probably be remote, somewhere off the grid. Maybe even in an area Roth had forgotten about. But not far enough that Rick couldn't keep an eye on me.

A place that reminded him of me, and me of him. Where I had been before. A place you might even find in a John Wayne movie.

I knew exactly where my husband was hiding.

Chapter 42

Rothsville hadn't changed much since August of 1977, the last time I had stepped foot in the Godforsaken town that looked right at home in the 1800's Wild West. Rows of crumbling brick buildings that used to be a shopping district, weeds overtaking patches of forlorn sidewalk, potholes the size of craters chewing away the road. An old Corbin Roth Real Estate sign survived, the Soviet-red background with gold lettering, straight from 1977, tattered but clinging to dear life. Only cockroaches and sewer rats looked like they had survived the aftermath of Corbin Roth's leadership here.

I hadn't slept a wink in days, but at my age, with my pleated stack of undereye wrinkles, no one would notice the difference. Driving aimlessly through the town, I guessed my way up and down random streets as my phone navigation went blank with no cell service.

Lost in an eerie, vacant town with no way to call for help? Had this been a movie, I would be screaming at the character to turn around and go home. But just like the character who does the exact opposite of what's safe and sane, I kept driving deeper into danger.

It seemed too much to hope for a coffee shop. Heck, I'd even settle for gas station coffee at this point.

The entire town looked forgotten. Only one building had a rusted-out truck parked—or abandoned—out front. Catching a glimpse of an actual live person moving inside, I was pleasantly shocked to see a sign of life as I pulled up to the same service area Rick and I had stopped at once upon a time. Except this time I wasn't riding a hog and heading to a rodeo in the hottest part of summer.

On what was left of the sidewalk, a motorcycle-shaped tarp blocked my way to the building. I lifted the bottom of the plastic drape and looked underneath. *Large Marge!* So Rick had to be somewhere around here.

A light glowed from inside the decrepit building, along with a neon OPEN sign in the window blinking uncertainly but buzzing emphatically. A single metal shelf sat crookedly in the middle of the gritty room, holding a random scattering of pre-packaged junk food next to automobile oil. The entire other side of the shelf was dedicated to cases of beer.

My shoes stuck to the encrusted tile as I stepped up to a glass counter displaying a variety of cigarettes, lighters, and hunting knives. Behind the counter an open door led into a back office, from which spirited banjo music played on a radio while a man hummed along. I was deep in rural no-man's-land.

"Hello?" I called out.

The gas station attendant wandered out of the back room, standing across from me at the counter wearing overalls that very well could have been from 1977. Heck, based on the waterfall of wrinkles falling down the guy's face, he may have even been the same person with that same brand of cigarette perched in his now-toothless mouth.

An open Budweiser left a ring of condensation on the glass

counter. Cold and newly opened. It was a mystery to me how anyone would want a smoke this early in the morning, let alone a beer. It wasn't yet five o'clock somewhere. The bigger mystery, though, was how he was still alive.

"Howdy there," he greeted. The cigarette—barely a nub—bobbed on his lip with each word. "You lost?"

It was a logical question, because I was pretty sure no one intended to ever find themselves in this dingy gas station in this dingy town.

"Not exactly. I'm looking for someone."

He grunted, put out the cigarette in an ashtray next to the cash register, then sipped his cold beer. "We ain't got no visitors in these parts, ma'am."

"It's my husband. I think he might be hanging out somewhere here in Rothsville, but I don't know where to look." I had selected the words *hanging out* carefully so as to not draw any undue suspicion. Unfortunately, no one hung out here, so it was instantly suspicious.

"Well, it sounds like you're tryin' to find someone who don't want to be found."

"So you *have* seen him?" I asked hopefully. "Because his bike's out front."

He didn't speak for a long moment. Police scanner chatter filled the awkward space between us. He reached next to the cash register, where the police scanner sat, and clicked it off.

"What if I have?"

Clearly he was going to make me work for any information. But I knew a quicker way to get things done. "Is it money you want? I don't have much, but maybe we could work something out."

He snickered. "You think I have use for money? I'm betting the man your husband is hiding from is the same one who owns this here town. He could easily have me killed for helping either of you."

So he *had* seen Rick.

"Sir, he would never find out, I swear." I dropped my voice to a conspiratorial whisper "I just want to get my husband and go. You'll never see or hear from us again. Please."

He scrutinized me with cloudy eyes, then set his beer down. I followed him along the counter to the end where a pot of coffee was brewing. Grabbing a Styrofoam cup, he poured it to the brim and handed it to me, along with a handful of sugars and packets of creamer that may or may not have been from the twenty-first century.

"It's on the house."

I was running on pure adrenaline, so I didn't care how long that coffee was sitting out. I would have accepted a caffeine IV if he offered it.

"Thanks."

I poured the sugars and creamer in, stirring it with the tiny plastic stick he gave me. He handed me a lid, which I popped on before gulping a mouthful, scrunching at the burned taste while he watched me.

"So will you tell me where he is or not?"

"Sorry I can't help you, ma'am."

The only option now was calling Detective Hughes for reinforcement. I suspected Rothsville was out of her jurisdiction, but maybe she could get in touch with the local department here.

"Do you know where I can get a cell phone signal around

here?" I asked.

I thought I saw his eyebrow raise, but his forehead, occupied by deep wrinkles, weighed it down too much to give much lift.

"Cell phone service? Do you know where you are, lady? We don't have that world wide web in these parts. But you can check the payphone around the side of the building to see if that still works. I probably have a quarter around here somewhere…"

He reached for a plastic tub filled with pennies that were useless in a payphone. I didn't want to expend the energy explaining the difference between cellular signals versus internet lines. Especially since I didn't know much about the differences either.

"No, that's okay. But thanks anyways."

I couldn't walk away. I had to get him talking, but how? If he didn't want money, what would a banjo-lovin' country fella like this want? What did all men want?

A second to nonstop sex, men wanted their names to live on forever. I would have rather let Rick die than give this man sex, but I could offer him a consolation prize.

After another tangy sip, I said, "What if I told you the man you're afraid of is dead? And you could be remembered as the one who took his entire criminal empire down."

"You sayin' you killed Corbin Roth?" He scoffed.

"I'm not saying I didn't."

He eyed me suspiciously. "What makes you think I care to be remembered by anyone?"

"Because no one wants to end up forgotten. '*It's not how you're buried; it's how you're remembered.*'"

253

His lips parted in what strained to be a grin. "John Wayne in *The Cowboys*. Well done, miss."

"What do you say? Will you tell me where my husband is, and I'll make sure you're never forgotten?"

"I still think you're lyin' about Roth, but if you did kill him, then I'd tell you to head over yonder," he pointed across the street to a vacant used car lot, "find your husband, and take him home… if he's still alive."

"What do you mean, if he's still alive?"

He shrugged a bony shoulder poking up under the overalls strap. "Let's just say you're not the only one who has been lookin' for your husband…"

His voice drained as he turned back to his office without another word, cranking up the radio as the DJ launched into the morning news.

I felt sick to my stomach.

Had someone gotten to Rick first?

Chapter 43

I bumbled my way across the street while tiny brown springs of coffee spit up out of the cup's lid hole. I stopped short of entering the empty used car lot building that was once owned by Roth but now owned by Mother Nature.

If someone dangerous knew Rick was here, I couldn't just walk into a potential trap with guns a'blazin' because first of all, I didn't have a gun. And second of all, I wasn't keen on getting killed. Stealth wasn't on my side, as my joints creaked and cracked, but what I lacked in agility I made up for in smarts. I had gotten this far, hadn't I?

I slunk around the back of the building, searching for a vehicle or any mode of transportation that indicated someone else was here. Nada. Not a car in sight. No cars hopefully meant no threat inside. I didn't think most killers took an Uber to and from their crime scenes.

Neither side of the building had any entrances—only a front and back door, and the back door was locked. It looked like there was only one way in… and one way out. So I headed to the front door, hoping whatever threat the gas station attendant had alluded to was long gone.

Newspapers taped to the wall of windows obscured any view inside. When I found a rock-sized hole punched through a windowpane near the door, I reached through and tore off a fistful of taped-up paper. I peeked inside, seeing nothing but an empty showroom. No furniture, no cars, no Rick.

All this lurking around had me breaking a sweat at this early-morning hour. In Bloodson Bay, summer usually held a tight lid on autumn all the way through October, until winter would snap and take charge until January. At this time of year it wasn't uncommon to bundle up in a sweater at dusk, then strip down to a swimming suit by dawn. The weather was more indecisive than Tara picking an outfit for girl's night out.

The glass front door had been shattered near the handle, where I assume Rick must have punched through the glass to unlock the door. It opened easily and quietly.

Despite the morning sun glowing through the newspaper shades, the interior was dim. Grime layered the walls. Cobwebs hung in ropy hoops from the ceiling. Bugs crunched beneath my feet on a sun-bleached tile floor, varnished with filth. In here, a gray dreariness seemed to be rising rather than the sun, as if gloom was the natural state.

Had Rick been squatting in this filth? It was no wonder the gas station attendant had questioned Rick's survival.

A short narrow hallway at the end of the former lobby took me further into the building, deep into an eerie darkness where little legs scurried across the floor, startling a robust scream from my lungs. So much for any chance of the element of surprise.

Puddles splashed with each step, where holes in the roof allowed pinpricks of light to seep through. When a critter ran across my feet, I jumped back, muffling my shriek with a hand over my mouth. I glanced down in time to see a large swamp rat scurry into the shadows… in the same direction I was heading. I shook away visions of rats feasting on Rick's half-chewed-off face.

At the end of the hallway I found several more rooms, former offices and all completely empty but one, where a rotted table and chairs had once stood erect but had since caved in. Against the back wall I saw a bundle of fabric. I stepped inside.

The blanket moved ever so subtly.

I gasped.

"Rick? Is that you?"

The mass of tattered cloths shifted, then slid down to the sticky tile floor. Underneath was a man, shivering and shaking and huddled in the corner.

"Rick!" I scurried to him, relieved to see he was alive. Barely.

"Gingersnap? Am I dreaming?"

I pressed my hand to his forehead. Cold, like death.

"No, it's really me, Rick. Are you hurt?"

Lifting his shirt, I found his stomach intact, with the faint scar from where he'd taken a knife to his gut last year. Both of his wrists were bound in a swathe of cloth torn from his t-shirt.

"What happened to your wrists?" I asked, noting the dried blood that had seeped through the wraps.

"Used glass to cut zip ties… caught my skin a little." Rick struggled to get the explanation out, which made a lot more sense than him chewing them off like I had imagined.

Other than his bandaged wrists, there were no other marks or injuries on his body. He looked fine… except he clearly wasn't fine.

I didn't see oozing blood, other than crusty dried crimson

beneath a cut in his cheek and under his nose, which hung at a slight bend that it hadn't had before. I touched the spot where the bone angled, and Rick winced and jolted back with a groan. Gunther had admitted to roughing him up, but breaking his nose? And they called each other friends! Though I knew Rick, who could be as stubborn as a mule, and several times in our marriage I would have enjoyed throwing a punch to his face.

The injuries explained the blood at the foot of the chair in the storage unit. I learned from the first time Rick had broken his nose that he was a bleeder.

"I'm… not… hurt." Speaking seemed to dagger him with each syllable.

"Sure you're not."

Weakly lifting his arm up, he held his hand out to me. He gripped something tightly, as if it kept him on the brink of life, but I couldn't tell what was tucked into his palm. As I reached to take it, he began to convulse in a fit of coughs and sputtered words, kicking the blanket off of him.

Kneeling closer to him, my knee met something sharp and jagged. I shifted aside. On the floor beside him were his motorcycle keys and a prescription bottle. I almost overlooked this little fact until I let it sink it.

When he had come back to drop off the pink carnations, he must have grabbed his sleeping pills. That could only mean he had no intention of returning.

He seizured again, this time foam pouring out of his mouth. I'd forgive him for everything if he would just be okay!

I scooped him into my arms. His body was frigid and damp. I needed to call 9-1-1, if I could find a cell phone signal. God only knew how long that would take, but I had no other choice but to try.

I patted my back pocket—empty.

My purse! I had left my useless phone in my purse in the front seat of my car.

I assessed Rick, wanting to carry him out the door with me right now, arm in arm, but I knew he would never make it. He was inching toward the shadows, and I feared if I left him— even for a moment—he would be walking among the dead when I returned.

"I have to leave you for just a few minutes to get my phone," I told him. "I need to try to call for help."

His hand shot out, grabbing me by the wrist. "No. Don't leave."

"I have to, Rick. You're dying and I don't know what happened to you," I tried to explain, but he clasped my wrist even tighter.

Why was he so pale? He couldn't have possibly lost that much blood from a nose bleed.

"Found… me," he muttered, the words coming out in strange slurs.

"Yes, I found you. You can come home. You're safe. Corbin Roth is either dead or in jail by now." At least I hoped so.

He weakly shook his head. "No… Roth… found."

I tried to decode what he was saying, but his words were tossed around too haphazardly to make sense. Maybe Rick was referring to the blonde Roth had hired to find and kill him. If so, she wouldn't succeed now.

"You mean Ekaterina? She's dead, honey."

He sighed in frustration. It was the only thing he said so far that I could interpret.

"I… know."

I understood that too. But if Rick was tied up in the storage unit, then hiding out here in Rothsville, how did he know the happenings in Bloodson Bay?

"How did you find out that she's dead, Rick?"

He closed his eyes, tears slipping out. I thought back to how she had died. Poisoning, the initial medical examination had determined. Could Rick have done that to her?

My mind went back to Rick's Xanax pills. Crushable tablets that could have easily been used to poison an unsuspecting woman who met with a mysterious man at a bar, according to witnesses. That's what the investigation turned up so far, but they had never confirmed the identity of the man she had met with.

I picked up the prescription bottle. Shook it.

Empty.

"You killed her." I didn't need to ask. I already know.

Rick's eyes drooped open, and his body straightened up. I could tell it took everything in him to sit upright and speak. "I had to… stop her. Roth paid her… to kill you."

"Roth was trying to force you to turn over the gem, wasn't he?"

Rick nodded. "I had… to protect you."

"So all of this—this whole disappearing act and killing Ekaterina—you did it for me," I stated.

"It's always been… for you," Rick looked at me with the same adoring gaze that always won me over. But it wasn't working this time. It had lost its magic.

"Was refusing to give Roth the gem protecting me? Because

I know what it is worth, Rick. You could have given him the gem and ended it all. But no, you wanted it for yourself."

Rick leaned forward with a groan. "No! Gem… gone. Don—"

But I was too angry to let him pour on more lies.

"Oh really? It's gone? You mean the gem that you're hiding in your fist right now?" I pointed to his closed hand, still keeping a secret inside. "You were planning on taking it and running off and using it to start a new life, weren't you?"

"Oh, Gingersnap… I love you so much. If only you knew…"

"I know plenty, Rick. What I *don't* know is why you value that damn jewel more than my life. Well, congratulations. You got your consolation prize because you've got your gem and you've got your freedom, since Roth is no longer a threat and there's no one else after you." My words were pouring out in shouts and sobs.

There was so much more I wanted to yell at him from the heart, about the regret he planted inside me and the hope he crushed, but the words became slippery things that slid out of my grasp.

"I'm turning you in, Rick. It's the right thing to do. You killed Ekaterina, you murdered Sloane's father, and you have to pay for your crimes. I hope you can forgive me, but I can never forgive you."

But he continued to shake his head. Was he denying the truth yet again? Then his whole body wobbled, followed by the entire room. Or was that me swaying? The room seemed to be growing as Rick shrunk.

"What is happening?" I cried, tipping over to my side.

Rick looked at the cup in my hand.

"Where did… you get that?"

I blinked Rick back into full size, but he kept getting caught in a haze. "At the gas station. Why?"

He leaned forward, slapping the cup to the floor, spilling the half-empty contents all over my clothes.

"Hey! I was drinking that!" I yelled. Or at least I thought I yelled, but the sound seemed muted and distant.

I crawled to the wall, searching for something to help lift me. Clawing against the mildewy plaster, I climbed up myself back to my disoriented feet.

A *tap tap tap* echoed somewhere behind me.

"He's coming!" Rick grappled with the blanket, scrambling his way toward me.

"Who's coming?"

"Ging… run!"

There was no running for me. Only dropping hard to the sticky floor.

Chapter 44

"You should not have drunk the coffee."

I had whirled around just as I fell, only catching a brief glimpse of the gas station attendant behind me wearing a contorted grin that revealed his mouth void of teeth. From out behind the counter, he appeared all skin and bones. Even with him being lopsided, I could take this geezer on with my eyes closed and my hands tied behind my back. But when I glanced down at my hands, they weren't there. In fact, my whole body had been replaced by the floor.

"You wanna fight, old man?" I slurred, suddenly not so sure now that I could win.

"Oh, honey, what's the point? You're already dead."

Dead? What was this crazy country bumpkin talking about?

And why did my face and neck feel like they were on fire? I scratched at my skin, feeling bumps pop up underneath my nails. I itched until it oozed, but it only made it worse.

"What did you... do to me?"

He could either read minds or I had said it aloud, because the next thing he said was, "Your coffee—it was poisoned. The same way I poisoned your hubby over there. You can thank him for the idea."

Damn my gut for leading me astray again! I should have

known no one actually served burned coffee... even if it was *on the house*.

"You wanna hear the irony in all this?" he continued, like a movie villain monologue.

I really didn't.

"I just heard on the radio news that Corbin Roth *is* dead. You weren't lyin'! Which means all of this was pointless. Now I gotta bury *two* bodies... and I ain't gonna get a dime for it. I should have just taken your offer instead."

The parts of me that had been keeping myself upright collapsed from exhaustion and vertigo at the sound of his horrid laughter ricocheting against the endless spinning black that threatened to suffocate me. I tried to blink the darkness away, but it was insistent. Insidious.

"Please... help me," I begged, hoping it wasn't already too late.

"Why should I let you live, when you're the reason my daughter is dead?" He swiped at a tear that got caught in a fold of skin.

"Wha—I don't understand." I wasn't sure which was more debatable—that I killed his kid, or that any woman on earth would reproduce with this man.

"Oh, I guess your hubby didn't fill you in on all the details."

I tried to shake my head, but against the floor it came across as more of a bobble.

"I'm the one who freed Rick from Stow Away, Don't Throw Away and offered him a hideout here."

"What's that... to do with... daughter?" I slurred, sounding more like Rick by the minute.

"My girl helped put Rick in there—that's how I knew where

he was. But then she got the grand idea that we take the gem for herself. That's how this whole mess started. But boy oh boy, Rick is a tough nut to crack. None of my natural charm worked to get him to tell me where that jewel was!"

Natural charm? He couldn't charm a snake out of a tree.

"I can't blame my girl for tryin' to build a better life for herself, but I can blame your hubby for killin' her."

My brain might have been foggy, but it hadn't gone kaput just yet. I rolled over onto my back to look at him, to watch his expressions beneath all those pleats of skin.

"So your daughter is—"

"*Vy umnehe, cham vyglyadite*," he said, before immediately translating, "That means 'You're smarter than you look.'"

"Russian," I realized as I spoke. "Kat's father."

"And a vengeful father at that. Rick killed my only child. You don't take a man's daughter from him. Especially a man who was in the Bratva."

"Does Roth… know?" Not that it mattered anymore. I was minutes away from the grave.

"Who do you think helped him design all those Commie-red and gold signs around town? And made him untouchable all these years? I never asked for money in return, just asylum for me and girl."

"And a million-dollar gem," I reminded him with the last bit of snark I had left.

"Well, that was only to help Ekaterina could start a new life. But anyway, I can't bring her back from the dead. So the next best thing is making sure you're up there with her to keep her company. Tell her *otetz* loves her…"

As I sank into the infinite ether, I never imagined that the coffee I couldn't live without would be the thing that ended up killing me.

Chapter 45

December 25, 1979

Although the wind whipped icy air at my bare cheeks, I didn't feel the cold. Nor did my rear feel the chilly sand nipping through the polyester fabric of my bohemian dress inspired by Stevie Nicks in the latest issue of *Cosmopolitan*. As I sat between Rick's legs, my back to his chest, his chin on my head, he warmed every cell in my body.

Perhaps for the last time.

"I'm sorry about how I reacted to your gift," I said, my words lost to a brash winter ocean.

"Don't apologize. You were right. That jewel wasn't you. I don't know what I was thinking," Rick murmured into my wildly waving hair that veiled my eyes. "I promise to do better, Gingersnap."

"About that…" I began.

We each held a cheap plastic stemware glass full of boxed wine that Rick had picked up at the grocery store for Christmas dinner. I sipped a mouthful, savoring the sugary sweetness that only bargain wine offered.

"I want a family, Rick. But you're… not yourself lately, and I don't know if you'll ever find yourself again."

I underplayed it, though. It hadn't been *lately.* It had been *years* of lately.

Rick was silent for a long time, and only the ocean had something to say.

"You would make an incredible mother, Ging. The best mother. You deserve a family… but not with me."

I shifted in his arms, turning around to face him. The same clouds that pushed the gale angled over the evening sunset, cleaving Rick's face into shadow and light.

"What are you saying? Do you… want a divorce?"

"It's not about what I want. It's about what you deserve. I can't help but fail you. It's all I know how to do. From the moment I didn't graduate high school, I knew it, and your parents knew it too. And I'll never stop failing you."

"Why not? You have choices, Rick. You can choose to do better—"

"No! I can't, Ging! That's the exact problem. I'm in too deep…"

"In too deep? In what too deep? What does that even mean?" I had a hint of an idea that he had been dabbling in some shady business dealings, but he had never confirmed it. And I had never wanted to know. Until now.

"I can't tell you. You'll never forgive me, and I can't live with that," he stated cryptically.

"What if I could forgive you? We could leave this town, start over somewhere new, and build our perfect family together. We could have our happily ever after, Rick."

His eyes brightened. "Are you serious? You'd leave Bloodson Bay with me and start an adventure together?"

I would have done anything for him, but he was too full of big ideas and empty promises and unfulfilled dreams that I never got to prove it to him. He clung too tightly to the big, idealistic visions that he never reached out for the small but stunning realities right in front of him.

Lifting my plastic stemware up for a toast, I clinked against his. "Cheers to adventure!"

Rick gulped his wine in a single swish, then tossed his glass on the beach and leaned in to kiss me. His mouth filled me with a sweet flavor of fruit as his tongue rolled around with mine. Every kiss grew hungrier, until something shifted.

This wasn't the memory I remembered anymore. It became something warped and unfamiliar. Twisted.

I leaned back, trying to push Rick away from me. But his lips were locked on mine, and I was filled with a lurching nausea that roiled in my belly. My chest cracked open, my breaths pinched shut, and my skin burned off.

I was coughing, vomiting, while Rick suffocated me with his mouth. Wild-eyed with fear, I tried to get him to look at me, see what he was doing to me, but his face disappeared into a blur. Then it morphed. The bones shifted, his features blended, and it was no longer Rick's mouth on mine. It was Gunther's.

Chapter 46

I woke up to a view of water-stained ceiling tiles. Followed by the pressure of fingers down my throat. Then coughing vomit up all over myself. And the cherry on top? Gunther Jones's lips pressing on my puke-crusted mouth as he pumped life into my chest.

It wasn't how I imagined our first kiss.

But I was alive, so I could live down the embarrassment.

"I would kiss you too," Tara's voice was the first one I heard, distant like in a dream, "but I don't have any breath mints on hand. What you're blowing out of that mouth is way worse than my Caesar salad breath."

Only Tara would pull me out from that shallow grave with an inappropriate joke at an inappropriate time. I had taught her well.

I tried to speak, but my muscles were too weak. My brain running too slow. So instead I blew in her face.

She laughed, waving my stink away. "I'm just glad you're back among the living, even if you don't smell like it!" Tara knelt over me, sobbing with a huge smile when I looked up at her upside-down face. She grabbed my hand. "You gave us quite a scare, Ging."

"Scarier than…" I coughed, finding it hard to push out more

than one word at a time, "my breath?"

I laid there on a nasty floor, under a spiderwebbed ceiling, in Gunther's arms, taking it all in. Letting each deep breath fill me. Tugging at the pieces of a mental puzzle that went missing. Something bad had happened, but I couldn't quite remember.

"Hey, you okay?" Tara asked, noticing my descent into worry.

The fringe hem of Tara's shawl hung over my face, tickling my cheek. I swatted it away, but it only returned with more fringes.

"I'm not entering the Pearly Gates before getting my shawl back that you're wearing." Words came easier now, but when I tried on a grin, it fell, too weak.

"I guess I'm keeping it, then." Tara wrapped the shawl around her and squeezed my palm, forcing her adoring gaze on me that made me feel uncomfortable with all the attention.

"Over my dead body," I retorted with a chuckle.

"Don't you dare!" she warned.

Another coughing fit shook me as I reoriented myself to my surroundings. I didn't recognize this place at first. And then the details slowly collected together like runoff in a sewage drain. Which was exactly what this place looked like.

Gunther raised me to a sitting position as I coughed air in and out of my lungs, but at least no puke. Another awkwardly adoring gaze came from him, and I shied away.

"What happened? I can't seem to remember…"

"I'm pretty sure you were poisoned," Gunther answered. "You had the same rash and vomit that Kat had when I found her…" He stopped mid-sentence, casting a concerned look at Tara. "But the police are on the way. Along with an ambulance.

You're going to be okay."

I shifted to look around, finding Gunther and Tara—then my gaze panned to Sloane—surrounding me. It was oddly serene. The restraint of their smiles. The solemn looks of sympathy. Gunther's lips parted, like he had more to say.

"How did you find me?" I asked.

"Good old-fashioned technology. Your cell phone's location sharing," Tara answered. I wasn't sure what location sharing was, but I was certainly glad for it.

"The cell service here sucks, but it at least clocked your cell phone location right outside of town, so we just drove around until we found your car across the street. From there we spread out until we found you… here."

Leaning forward, I skimmed the room, looking for someone. I couldn't remember who.

"Are you looking for the guy who poisoned you?" Gunther guessed. But that wasn't who I was looking for.

"He ran off just as we got here," Tara explained. "He tricked us by telling us he just found you like this and offered to call for help, but when we went back to look for him he was gone."

"Let him go. Living here, he's had a hard enough life as it is." And like me, he had lost a child. I couldn't punish a man who just went through that, even if he did just try to kill me. "Based on the way he smoked like a chimney," and I couldn't forget the breakfast beer, "he probably doesn't have much time on earth left. I'm fine letting nature take him out."

But I wasn't concerned with the gas station attendant. Rick was who I was searching for. I tried to peer around the wall of legs around me toward where I remembered Rick sitting, but Sloane knelt beside me, blocking my view. She exchanged a look with Tara, a look that spoke a tragic story.

"Rick?" I forced my mouth to utter.

I shoved Gunther aside, pushing my way through Sloane and Tara. Rick lay slouched against the wall, sleeping. Only… he wasn't. His chest wasn't moving, his position wasn't right. His face was gray, his lips crusted in white. I grabbed his hands, which flopped out of mine. Cool and lifeless.

Out of his hand something fell onto his lap. A photo—one taken so long ago that I wouldn't have even remembered it if it hadn't been for that empty picture frame Tara had found.

It had to be in early 1986, before Rick had left for good. Taken when Benson was thigh-high, and Jonah couldn't have had his first birthday yet. I was pregnant with Chris at the time, and the four of us were standing in the surf outside our tiny beach house, when life was poor but simple and perfect.

In matching neon tracksuits, Rick held Benson and I held Jonah with Rick's hand resting on my tiny baby bump. And we all held each other. I couldn't remember who had taken the picture, but I remembered how easy it was to smile back then. How could we not smile when our outfits looked like life-sized glowsticks?

Rick must have removed the photo out of the frame when he broke out of the storage unit, dropped off the carnations, and disappeared. This was what he had held on to as he died—not the gem like I had thought, but our memories.

Something he had tried to tell me about the gem as he was dying struck me differently now.

"Gem gone. Don—" he had begun to say before I had cut him off. The gem—I had a feeling I knew where it was, and Rick knew who would benefit most from it.

He had tried to do the right thing in the end, a last hurrah to prove his love, but I hadn't let him. I didn't know he was capable of something good. But I would carry out Rick's plan for the gem that Sloane didn't want and carried too much pain for Alika. All of the suffering and loss around it wouldn't be in vain.

It was a comfort that in his last moments, Rick chose me. He gave me his heart. Even if that heart was no longer beating.

More than anything I wanted to share a cheap box of wine together on the beach, listening to his big empty dreams about whisking me away on an adventure we would never take, swaying home tipsy and fulfilling. But that wish was lost at sea.

I felt the warmth of two bodies standing sentry beside me, as if protecting me from the darkness of this hour. Sloane and Tara both dropped down to me, one on each side, wrapping me in their friendship.

Sloane said nothing, only held me. Which she was so good at doing.

Tara sighed, then cupped my hand. "Hey, Ging. I'm sorry Rick didn't make it. I really am."

It took a long time for the words to settle. So long that by the time I think I actually heard her, the EMTs had already arrived, followed by the police. The chaos of the medical intervention, and police questions, and vital sign readings made me forget all about Rick's death.

Until I remembered again. And again. And again.

Rick was dead. Rick was dead. Rick was dead.

Gunther walked alongside the stretcher that the EMTs lifted me onto, then wheeled toward the ambulance.

"I tried to save Rick—for you. I'm sorry I was too late," he consoled.

"Maybe it's better this way."

I hated myself for thinking it, but Rick and I were complicated. Caught in a toxic, possessive love that was doomed to end in death. But at least we had our closure. Maybe tomorrow I would cry until the tears dried to salt. But for today I would let myself forget.

"Does this mean you're going to follow through on that brinner date you promised?" My grin muscles had gotten their strength back.

Gunther kissed my forehead, then rubbed his hand along my hair. "Not until my jail time is up."

"Jail time?"

"I'm turning myself in, Ginger. Corbin Roth is dead and no longer a threat. But I have a lot of… associates. So I'm going to help clean up Bloodson Bay and put Ewan Valance where he belongs—behind bars with me. I know where all the bodies are buried. I'm going to make sure he pays for those crimes."

I was surprised he would actually follow through with something. I wasn't used to seeing that from Rick.

"Why are you doing this?"

"You were right. I have a choice to make and this is the right one. I'm going to finish what Rick started."

"I guess this would make you one of the good guys."

"I would like to one day believe that." He kissed me on the cheek one last time, then the EMT lifted my gurney into the back of the truck.

"Take care of yourself while I'm gone, okay?" Gunther called out to me.

I lifted a thumbs-up, realizing maybe I wasn't quite ready for the modern dating scene after all.

Tara filled in the space beside me that Gunther vacated as he approached a uniformed officer, who began taking his statement.

"Here's your cell phone for you to take with you to the hospital so you can call me if you need anything. I'll follow you in my truck, and Sloane will drop your car off at your house."

My friends thought of everything. How did I get so lucky to have them?

As if suddenly waking up from a cell-service-less coma, my phone pinged with a slew of new texts and email messages. I opened my email first, finding at the top of my inbox the DMV email address of my friendly neighborhood customer service agent who had been researching the title for Rick's motorcycle:

I hope some good news helps you feel a little better today as you fight that Mad Cow Disease. I'm happy to report that there is only one other owner of the motorcycle you are looking for, so it should make tracking down your bike a little easier. The title transfer I found was between Rick Mallowan to Gunther Jones. Good luck being reunited. And stay away from the bright light!

Gunther was in the middle of being handcuffed when I looked over at him, meeting his sorry, lyin'-eyes gaze. So he had beat the crap out of Rick not just once, but twice, and I couldn't help but feel a tiny prick of pride that it was over *me*.

Luckily I had sworn off men forever, because my worth didn't come from Ricks or Gunthers. I was a proud member of

Tara's Angels, surrounded by whip smart women who were tougher than a $2 steak.

As the ambulance rumbled off to the hospital, I reflected on the moral of my story. Never trust a bartender in cowboy boots, because he'll turn out to be a bull-riding cowboy who will feed you nothing but bull.

Chapter 47

BLOODSON BAY BULLETIN

FATHER-SON KIDNAPPERS REUNITE OVER $1 MILLION GEM

Judge Ewan Valance will be sharing a jail cell with his son Leonard Valance for the next twenty-five years to life, after a witness came forward with incriminating evidence that the unjust justice was in fact behind multiple crimes.

The list is extensive, including drug trafficking, theft, murder, and the 1995 kidnapping of Alika Apara. As well as coercing his underage son Leonard, who was a teenager at the time of the abduction, to aid and abet the kidnapping and torture of Apara.

What brought the gavel down on this Machiavellian magistrate? A rare gemstone.

Working alongside the recently deceased Corbin Roth, whose ties to the Russian Bratva had been exposed, former judge Ewan Valance was incriminated in covering up the attempted armed robbery of a gem worth over $1 million dollars, which resulted in several deaths, including Apara's husband. Ewan Valance won't be seeing daylight anytime soon.

The gem was recently recovered in a donation box dropped off at the Loving Arms Children's Home donation center. After requests to the public for the original owner of the jewel to come forward went unanswered, the gem was auctioned off and raised over $800,000 for the orphanage.

When administrators tracked down the donation box to the deceased Benson Mallowan, whose name was written on the box, Mallowan's mother came forward to comment, stating that "it was the destiny of the gem to help the kids."

"A chunk of jewelry is not worth anything if it's not bringing joy to others," she stated in an interview. "My husband Rick Mallowan died trying to leave behind some good in the world and he wanted this gem, with all its dark past, to do something positive in the end. Rick died trying to right his wrongs, and I hope this gem does exactly that for the children's home."

Thanks to this generous contribution, a fall festival, hosted by Sloane Apara's Feel the Noize Party Planning, will help the kids celebrate the offerings and renovations that will be coming to Loving Arms Children's Home, including new services available for Deaf and hard-of-hearing children.

My two best friends, Sloane and Tara, sat on my living room sofa, which now had plenty of available cushion space after Tara helped me declutter all day. As I read the newspaper article aloud and proud, I added a little extra theatrical emphasis, but we didn't applaud too enthusiastically, since Peace had joined us for a hug-it-out night of bonding and board games. We didn't want to rub it in her face that her boyfriend was no better than my husband.

"I'm not mad anymore," Peace assured me. "Who knows. Maybe once he's done his time we can see where things go."

Tara cocked an eyebrow at me, and I knew what she was hinting at: Gunther Jones.

"Don't even say it, Tara," I warned. "No more ex-cons for me. At least for now."

As I set out the board game Trouble—aptly named for our group—laughter and wine (non-alcoholic for Tara) flowed freely all around, with assurances that we would never let bro's come before ho's ever again.

**

There's more murder, mayhem, and mystery brewing in Bloodson Bay that only Tara's Angels can solve in *Tell Me What She Knows*, the next book in the IF ONLY SHE KNEW MYSTERY SERIES!

If you haven't read the whole series yet, you can grab it at **www.pamelacrane.com**. While you're there, sign up for my newsletter to get notified when the next book in the series is available for preorder, along with a chance to grab a free early release copy.

WHAT SHE DOESN'T KNOW

About the Author

PAMELA CRANE is a *USA Today* bestselling author and wrangler of four kids who rescues horses and has a writing addiction. She lives on the edge and writes on the edge... where her sanity resides. Her thrillers unravel flawed women with a villainous side, which makes them interesting... and perfect for doing crazy things worth writing about. When she's not cleaning horse stalls or cleaning up after her kids, she's plotting her next murder.

Join her newsletter to get a free book and updates about her new releases and deals at **www.pamelacrane.com**.

Enjoy What You Read?

A Karin Slaughter Killer Reads Pick:
Little Deadly Secrets

The deadliest secrets lie closest to home...

From *USA Today* bestselling author Pamela Crane comes an addictively readable domestic suspense novel about friendship, motherhood ... and murder.

Three best friends. Two unforgiveable sins. One dead body.

Mackenzie, Robin, and Lily have been inseparable forever, sharing life's ups and downs and growing even closer as the years have gone by. They know everything about each other. Or so they believe.

Nothing could come between these three best friends . . .
Except for a betrayal.

Nothing could turn them against each other . . .
Except for a terrible past mistake.

Nothing could tear them apart . . .
Except for murder.

Milton Keynes UK
Ingram Content Group UK Ltd.
UKHW040627170124
436182UK00001B/16